UPRISING AT DAWN

Between Two Flags

1. *Cry of Courage*
2. *Where Bugles Call*
3. *Burden of Honor*
4. *Road to Freedom*
5. *Uprising at Dawn*
6. *Risking the Dream*

An American Adventure

1. *The Overland Escape*
2. *The Desperate Search*
3. *Danger on Thunder Mountain*
4. *The Secret of the Howling Cave*
5. *The Flaming Trap*
6. *Terror in the Sky*
7. *Mystery of the Phantom Gold*
8. *The Gold Train Bandits*
9. *High Country Ambush*

LEE RODDY

BETHANY HOUSE PUBLISHERS
MINNEAPOLIS, MINNESOTA 55438

Cover by illustration by Chris Ellison
Cover design by Lookout Design Group, Inc.

Published by Bethany House Publishers
A Ministry of Bethany Fellowship International
11400 Hampshire Avenue South
Minneapolis, Minnesota 55438
www.bethanyhouse.com

Printed in the United States of America by
Bethany Press International, Minneapolis, Minnesota 55438

Library of Congress Cataloging-in-Publication Data
Roddy, Lee, 1921–
Uprising at dawn / by Lee Roddy.
p. cm. — (Between two flags ; 5)
Summary: Gideon, a farm boy living in Virginia during the Civil War, overhears three men plotting a slave rebellion.
ISBN 0–7642–2029–2 (pbk.)
[1. Slavery—Fiction. 2. United States—History—Civil War, 1861–1865—Fiction.] I. Title.
PZ7.R6 Up 2000
[Fic]—dc21 99–051012

To Mrs. Sue Smead

and her

fifth-grade students

at

Forest Lake Christian School,

Auburn, California

LEE RODDY is the award-winning and bestselling author of many books, television programs, and motion pictures, including *Grizzly Adams*, *Jesus*, and THE D.J. DILLON ADVENTURES SERIES, BHP's AN AMERICAN ADVENTURE, and Focus on the Family's THE LADD FAMILY SERIES. He and his wife make their home in California.

CONTENTS

PROLOGUE

From Gideon Tugwell's journal, October 19, 1933

Having passed my eighty-fifth birthday, I find it especially helpful to open the pages of my journal written when I was a boy growing up during the Civil War.

Words set down so long ago stir memories of joy and sadness, of growing and learning, of excitement and danger as the conflict raged between North and South.

There were deeply personal risks for three of us in Virginia that September of 1862, when our Confederate troops invaded Maryland and Abraham Lincoln issued his official Emancipation Proclamation to free some slaves. That was the historical background for the personal perils that suddenly engulfed Emily Lodge, Nat Travis, and me, and had us struggling for our very lives.

Emily was an orphaned Northerner trapped in the South when the conflict erupted. Nat was a slave boy who unexpectedly encountered not only great physical jeopardy, but the most emotional period of his life. I, the boy Gideon, was a dirt farmer's son with a dream in my heart.

Glancing at my old journal, I see that there was no hint of our coming troubles one quiet Sunday afternoon. But that quickly changed. Here's how it began. . . .

A PLOT IN THE SWAMP

September 14, 1862, near Church Creek, Virginia

Gideon moved quietly through the silent swamp that Sunday afternoon, searching for his family's big black hog that had recently escaped its pen. That's when the boy heard a low murmur of voices.

Gideon stopped to listen, knowing that few people ever ventured into Black Water Swamp, home to countless dangers from bears, poisonous snakes, and treacherous peat bog. He remembered tales of runaway slaves who got lost in the mire where their bones were later found.

Standing still caused Gideon's old work brogans to promptly start sinking into the spongy peat. Even though it was mid-September and the peat had dried somewhat, it was as shaky as a spoonful of his mother's apple jelly. From under his black slouch hat that only partly covered his straw-colored hair, Gideon peered through blue eyes to locate the source of the voices. *Over there,* he told himself, focusing on a stand of red maple trees. *Sounds like slave dialect. But why are they here?*

Gideon knew there were two possibilities: Either they had escaped from their masters and were hiding, or they had taken advantage of Sundays off to slip away from a tobacco plantation without their owners' permission. Whether runaways or not, they were not supposed to be in the swamp. They would not like a white boy spying on them because he would surely report them to a slave catcher or brutal white "pattyrollers." The masters would also severely whip captured runaways.

Gideon's common sense warned him to slip away, but curiosity prompted him to ease toward the men. He carefully lifted his feet from the muck, aware that the canopy of trees had shut out the sun, creating an eerie sense of danger. He ignored the stench of stagnant water and decaying vegetation while avoiding countless thorny vines and shrubs that snagged at his rough farm clothes.

Keeping a large black gum-tree trunk between him and the low murmur of voices, he skirted a thick growth of greenbrier vine with its sharp thorns. He slipped up behind the tree. There he stopped, removed his hat so the brim wouldn't show, and warily peered around the trunk.

Beyond a dense clump of underbrush that partially blocked his vision, Gideon saw three black men on a small hummock that kept their feet out of the bog. Two sat on a fallen log with their backs to Gideon. They listened to a big, wide-shouldered man whose face was blocked from Gideon's view.

This man's voice rose angrily. "I'se t'ared o' waitin' fer Massa Lincum's bluecoats to set us free! Now's de time to burn de big house down, an' don't leave no white fokes alive!"

"Dat's de way!" one of the seated men exclaimed, slapping a hand on his knee. "Fust, we gits all dem at de big house, den dem po' white trash neighbors. An we does it dis month!"

Terror made goose bumps pop up on Gideon's arms. *He means us Tugwells and Briarstone!* Horrified, he drew his head back, alarmed for his family and his good friend, Emily Lodge, of nearby Briarstone Plantation.

I've got to warn everyone! Gideon quietly but hurriedly headed back the way he had come. He glanced back without breaking stride and blundered into a trailing greenbrier vine. "Ouch!" he exclaimed as the cruel barbs snagged his shirt sleeve and cut his arm.

Shouts erupted behind him, and then a sharp command.

Gideon ignored his bleeding arm to frantically rip his shirt sleeve free. Hearing the men chasing after him, he broke into a terrified run toward his home.

★ ★ ★ ★ ★

Pretty Emily Lodge perched on the side of the canopied four-poster bed and absently watched her cousin. Julie was a model Southern girl: soft-spoken, well-mannered, and submissive, especially around her domineering father and older brother. She stood in front of the mirror brushing her shoulder-length black hair. Her new maid, Massie, usually did that, but today she had been dismissed so the girls could talk of personal matters.

Without turning around, Julie asked, "Now that we're both almost fourteen, do you think much about a beau?"

Emily didn't answer. She thoughtfully contemplated her situation. Her siblings had died in 1860 and her parents last year. Emily had no choice but to move to the Confederacy to stay with her only living relatives. Yet Emily's great desire was to return to her rural hometown of Hickory Grove and her best friend, Jessie Barlow.

So far, Emily's repeated attempts to go back had failed. She was disappointed, yet she felt confident that it was God's will for her to remain in Virginia, at least for now. However, as Christmas approached, she felt homesick and again began to think of Illinois.

"Well?" Julie repeated. "Do you think about a beau?"

"Uh . . . not really," Emily said evasively. She was well developed and very attractive with fair skin and a small nose, mouth, and ears. She wasn't sure how she felt about boys, but both she and her cousin lately spent a lot of time grooming themselves and trying different hairstyles. Emily was uncomfortable having a maid do her hair, so Julie had created full Grecian curls at the back of her cousin's golden locks.

"What about Gideon?" Julie persisted, again running the brush through the cascade of glistening tresses.

"We're friends." Emily slid off the bed and walked to the second-story window. Her violet eyes skimmed over the yellow-leaf tobacco plants toward the Tugwells' small dirt farm and Black Water Swamp beyond.

"Then how about Brice Barlow?" Julie asked.

Emily felt a slight flush touch her cheeks. Before the war, she had seen a lot of Jessie Barlow's older brother, Brice, back in Illinois, where the handsome teen had jokingly said he was going to someday marry her. *Or was he serious?* Emily wondered.

She told Julie, "Brice and I are also friends."

"But what about when this cruel war is over?" Julie wanted to know. She laid the brush down on the dresser and came to stand beside Emily. "Then what?"

Emily's mind wasn't on such matters. She turned to her cousin. "Will your brother really sell Nat into the Deep South?"

"Of course. When servants repeatedly run away and don't stop even after they're whipped, there's nothing else to do. Nat will be sold so far down South that it'll be almost impossible for him to ever escape again."

Emily cringed at the word "servant." She said gently, "I can never call a slave a servant. A servant is free to come and go, but slaves—"

Julie broke in. "Let's not discuss that again! You'll always be a Yankee, and I'm always going to be a loyal Confederate. So let's just talk about beaus."

Emily shook her head. The only secret she had kept from Julie was the fact that she and Gideon had helped Nat escape from Briarstone the first time. She explained to Julie, "I think I'll ask your brother to change his mind and not—"

"Too late!" Julie interrupted. "William not only kicked Nat out of the big house after this second escape but sent him to the fields. This morning I heard William tell Mama he had sent for the speculator to sell him."

Emily's eyebrows shot up in surprise. "Already? But it's only been a few days since the slave catcher brought Nat back. And I don't blame him for trying to escape."

"Well, William disagrees, and he's in charge as long as Papa is away fighting those invading Yankees. Let's not talk about things beyond our control."

"I'm going to go talk to William about it right now." Emily headed toward the door.

"It won't do you any good!" Julie warned.

"Maybe not, but I've got to try," Emily replied, opening the door quickly. "Oh!" she exclaimed, startled at seeing Julie's maid straightening up.

Julie exclaimed, "Massie! You know better than to peek through a keyhole or try listening to white folks!"

"Yes, Miz Julie," the light-brown-skinned girl replied, her eyes downcast.

"Don't ever do it again!" Julie commanded sternly. "Now, get in here and tidy up!"

Massie curtsied and entered her young mistress's bedchamber as Emily hurried down the hallway. She briefly wondered if Massie had really been spying, but the thought was quickly replaced by planning how she might persuade William to change his mind about selling Nat.

★ ★ ★ ★ ★

Gideon ran for his life through the gloomy swamp. He dodged brush, leaped over fallen logs, and tripped over an exposed root. He sprang instantly and dashed on toward his family's farm, which was adjacent to the swamp.

His lungs soon burned from exertion, and his breath came in great, ragged gasps, but he dared not slow up. The men were gaining on him. He could hear their furious shouts close behind him and the sounds of their feet sloshing through the shallow pools of stagnant water.

Gideon knew that his would-be captors could not risk letting him escape. Even though he had not seen any of their faces, they didn't know that. If his pursuers caught him in the swamp, he suspected that not even his bones would ever be found.

The belief kept the blood surging through his body and gave him endurance beyond what he had ever known. Still, the soft, wet, sponge-like peat sucked at his feet, slowing every step and threatening to again throw him facedown into the marsh.

The shouts from his pursuers had now spread out. One was still directly behind him. The other two men were off to the sides, and all three were gaining on him. He briefly considered trying to hide, but those men were too desperate to stop looking for him. His only hope lay in reaching his home.

Panting hard from his run, Gideon was grateful that he and his father had hunted the swamp enough that Gideon could keep his sense of direction.

As he dashed by a clump of bushes, a large black bear appeared out of nowhere. The animal gave a startled *woof* and crashed away through the underbrush. Gideon risked a look back and was relieved to see the bear swerve and bound off in the direction Gideon had come. He heard a squeal of fright and shouts.

"B'ar!" one pursuer shrieked. "A b'ar! B'ar!"

Gideon heard a roar from the animal and wild crashing through the swamp. Clutching his chest, he staggered tiredly on, encouraged by shrieks of the three men, which made it clear to Gideon that they were suddenly all running in different directions away from him, trying to escape the bear. Soon after, Gideon wobbled toward the back door of his family home. With an effort he called, "Mama! Mr. Fletcher! Come quick! Slaves are plotting an uprising! They're going to burn Briarstone and kill everyone, including us!"

★ ★ ★ ★ ★

In the Briarstone carriage house, Nat Travis turned his head to squint at the gray-haired carriage driver. The movement made a small bell tinkle from where it was suspended above Nat's head at the end of a short, curved metal piece that stuck out from an iron collar padlocked around his neck. William Lodge, Nat's young owner, had ordered the uncomfortable collar and bell so that Nat's presence would always be known. It would not be easy to run away again.

Trying to sound casual yet convincing, Nat told the older man, "You're just guessing, Uncle George."

George scratched his curly white hair and thoughtfully studied the tall, slender slave boy whose mulatto skin and Caucasian features testified to his white father. George said with a disarming smile, "I'm just an old slave who's talking to pass the time."

Like Nat, he spoke without a trace of the common slave dialect. Only Nat knew that George could use proper English as well as he. In spite of the law forbidding it, Nat's first master had secretly educated him. George had taught himself to speak properly by copying the white people he had overheard while driving them many places.

George added, "Remember when you first came here a couple of years ago?"

"Yes, of course." As the newly purchased body slave to young Master William, Nat had not told a single person about his plans to escape to freedom. But George had somehow sensed his intentions and warned him to never trust anyone, not even another slave. That had been good advice, which Nat had heeded. He had come to respect and like Uncle George, but Nat still didn't share with him his innermost thoughts.

George said, "You've run twice, Nat. Once with that pretty girl Sarah, then again on your own. Both times young Master William nearly whipped you to death." George shook his grizzled head. "Now you wear that collar and bell. Still, it seems like some of us just got to keep trying for freedom, no matter what the cost. I see it in your eyes; you're thinking of doing it again."

It was true. On his last short time of freedom, Nat had heard that his eleven-year-old brother, Amos, was in bondage at a nearby small plantation. Nat intended to find Amos and escape together on the Underground Railroad, but first he had to get rid of the collar and bell.

That desire was intensified since Nat had been demoted from the big house to field-hand work under the merciless direction of Julius, Briarstone's slave driver. He hated Nat with a passion because of Sarah's escape.

Although slaves could not officially marry, last year Julius had planned to "jump over the broom" with Sarah. Instead, she and Nat escaped together. She was now safe in Canada, thanks to Emily Lodge and a "conductor" for the local but secret Underground Railroad. Nat, recaptured and sent to the fields, was now under Julius's direct supervision.

Nat had never told anyone about Emily's or Gideon's part in his first escape, just as he was sure they had never told anyone, not even their own relatives.

After a moment's reflection about the admonition to never

trust anyone, Nat shook his head. "Uncle George, you're still guessing."

"Oh, I don't want you to tell me, Nat. But the reason I mentioned it is because I heard something today when I was driving the young master in the carriage."

Sensing something important in the man's tone, Nat forced himself to sound only mildly interested. "Oh?"

George leaned forward and lowered his voice, even though there was no one else around. "William isn't going to give you a chance to run. He's sent for the speculator."

Nat flinched at the unexpected news. "To sell me?"

"All the way down to the mouth of the Mississippi River, where very few slaves ever escape to freedom. Most die in a few years of fever or being worked to death."

Nat couldn't hide his alarm. "When is he coming?"

"In the next few days."

Fighting sudden panic, Nat quickly stood up. "I have to think," he said and hurried away with the bell jangling.

A SECRET REVEALED

Panting hard and gasping for breath, Gideon had reached the back door when his mother jerked it open.

"What're you yelling about?" she asked anxiously, wiping flour from her hands onto her faded yellow apron.

"Some slaves are plotting an uprising!"

"What?" Her eyes opened wide in alarm, and her voice rose sharply. "How do you know?"

He collapsed on the homemade wooden bench and leaned across the matching kitchen table. "I heard them," he puffed. "I was looking for our hog in the swamp. There were three of them, and they chased me!"

"Mercy!" Martha Tugwell, a small woman with gray-streaked hair, turned toward the kitchen door. She peered out the window at the top half. "I don't see anyone."

"I got away!" Gideon leaped to his feet, his heart still pounding violently. "They're going to burn our place and Briarstone, and not leave any white people—"

"Hush!" His mother said firmly. "Keep your voice down! Ben and the girls are playing on the front porch." She quickly entered the adjacent front room and peered out the window to check on Gideon's two younger sisters and a brother.

Gideon asked, "What'll we do, Mama?"

She quickly returned to him. "First, tell me the whole thing—exactly who you saw and what was said."

He was just finishing retelling his story when heavy footsteps sounded on the back porch. Gideon jumped up to face the door. "It's them, Mama!"

"No, that's Mr. Fletcher's footstep." She hurriedly crossed to the door and opened it.

A former Confederate soldier, Shenandoah farmer, and a widower who had lost his left hand at the Battle of First Manassas, John Fletcher cleaned mud from his boots on the metal scraper. He stopped, sudden concern showing in his light blue eyes. "Something wrong, Martha?"

She nodded and motioned him inside. "Never mind the dirt. Come in and listen to what Gideon has to say."

Gideon was breathing normally again when he completed his second hurried telling. Fletcher looked down from his nearly six-foot height and laid his callused right hand on the boy's shoulder. "Did they say when or where, Gideon?"

"No. Well, wait! One of them said this month. I understand that they'd start with Briarstone, then come after us."

Fletcher shook his head. "This month still has sixteen days left in it. Not knowing exactly when they plan to attack means we've got no time to lose."

Martha Tugwell agreed. "We must warn the Lodges." She turned to Gideon. "Take the mule and ride hard to Briarstone. But be careful. Just because you didn't recognize those men doesn't mean that they don't know who you are."

The boy got to his feet. "I'll be careful, Mama."

She cautioned, "Don't say anything to your sisters or brother or tell anyone at Briarstone except your friend Emily and her family! There's no telling if some of the household slaves are part of this Rebellion."

"Hurry!" Fletcher urged. "We don't want another Nat Turner tragedy."

Gideon sprinted across the yard toward the barn, remembering what he had heard about Nat Turner. Thirty-one years ago, Turner had led a Virginia slave uprising where fifty-five white men, women, and children were killed. Upwards of two hundred black people also lost their lives in the backlash of crushing the rebellion.

★ ★

Gideon shuddered at the thought of what could happen if the three unknown plotters he had overheard carried out their plot. *Please, Lord,* he silently prayed, *don't let anything happen to any of us—or Emily!*

★ ★ ★ ★ ★

Emily knocked on the closed library door, still trying to think how best to ask her cousin William not to sell Nat into the Deep South. Hearing William's invitation, she entered the cozy room filled with books and the fragrance of fine leather.

At seventeen, William Lodge was solidly built with well-muscled arms and big hands. He didn't look up from where he was reading in his father's big wingback chair. Levi, the young body servant who had replaced Nat, stood unobtrusively off to the side. He did not look at Emily.

William asked bluntly, "What is it?"

"Uh . . . could we talk privately?"

"You can talk in front of Levi."

"No, not really," she said, hoping she wasn't hurting the slave's feelings.

For the first time, William looked up from his book. He seemed to sense something in her face that made him motion for Levi to leave.

As he exited, Emily's eyes swept the three walls covered with glass-fronted bookcases that protected dozens of leather bound volumes. Two windows flanked the small fireplace on the fourth wall, with matching wing chairs below each window.

Emily took a deep breath and came directly to the point. "William, I'm here to ask—"

"What's that commotion?" he interrupted.

Emily heard loud voices down the hall toward the front door. She recognized the calm, controlled words of Jason, whose duties included greeting guests at the front door. "Please wait here while I announce your presence."

Another voice protested, "There's no time to wait!"

"That's Gideon!" Emily exclaimed, alarmed at the unusual urgency and loudness of his tone. She rushed out of the library into the hall. "Jason! Let him in!"

Red-faced, William sputtered, "Emily!"

"Sorry," she said, knowing that William should have been the one to invite Gideon in, but she had acted impulsively because of Gideon's obvious distress. She lifted the hoopskirt above her ankles to walk faster.

In muddy clothes and shoes, Gideon pushed by Jason.

Emily cried in alarm, "Gideon! What is it?"

He ran toward her and William, who had followed her into the hallway. In a hoarse whisper, Gideon said, "I've got to talk to you both right away—alone!"

William glanced at Gideon's distraught face, then motioned toward the library. "In here."

As quickly as Gideon and Emily entered the library, William closed the door and Gideon blurted out his story.

A cold chill seized Emily. "That's horrible!"

"Yes," William said thoughtfully, "But with all the men away at war, a slave uprising is what almost every plantation family in the South fears most." He glanced at Gideon. "You're sure you can't identify any of them?"

"I didn't see their faces."

"How about their voices?" William asked.

"I'm not sure," Gideon admitted.

William said thoughtfully, "They had to have been from here."

Emily involuntarily sucked in her breath. "Here?"

William didn't answer her but looked at Gideon. "From what you said, I'm convinced they have to be my property. Probably field hands, but there could be a spy here inside this house, too."

Emily remembered catching Massie listening outside Julie's bedchamber door. "Is that possible, William?"

"Very possible, but that's not so bad because servants can't keep secrets. If there's a spy in this house, and one other person knows it, one of the servants will tell me for a little trinket or some other reward."

Emily didn't share the apparent quiet confidence that William had. She forced herself to ask calmly, "What'll we do?"

★ ★

William didn't answer for a moment. When he did, his voice was no longer that of an angry teen, but the master of a large plantation. "We'll do what I think our father would do if he were here instead of off fighting Yankees. We'll stop this uprising before it happens."

"How?" Gideon asked.

"Yes, how?" Emily echoed.

William didn't seem to hear. He asked Gideon, "Who else knows about this?"

"Just my mother and Mr. Fletcher, the man who helps on our farm."

"Good." William sounded pleased. "Only five of us know, so let's keep it that way. I won't even tell my mother or Julie. Mother is too ill to handle any more hard problems, and Julie doesn't need to know. I'll work out a plan to protect Briarstone by myself."

"Gideon said those men also mentioned his family, too," Emily reminded him.

Gideon didn't expect any help from William, who wanted the Tugwells' rich bottomland for himself. It was a goal he had inherited from his father.

Gideon said hastily, "I didn't come here for you to help us; I came only to warn you."

Emily gave him a brief but warm smile.

William mused, "Since you're the only one who was there to overhear them plotting, perhaps we should all work together on this problem."

Gideon hadn't expected that. "Uh . . . I'll need to talk to Mama and Mr. Fletcher. . . ."

"Of course." William walked quietly to the door and opened it suddenly as though checking to make sure nobody was listening. He closed it and faced Gideon and Emily. "But for the moment, I want you to tell me again exactly everything you heard and saw. Go ahead."

Gideon looked at Emily, uncertain whether to trust William's suspiciously agreeable behavior.

Emily nodded encouragingly and leaned forward to hear it

again. She had totally forgotten about asking her cousin not to sell Nat.

★ ★ ★ ★ ★

After leaving George, Nat headed toward the woods so he could be alone. *Only a few days before the trader comes,* he mused, trying to ignore the annoying bell on his collar. *I've got to run before then. But how?*

He passed the barn where last night the slaves had been permitted a dance. Sunday was their only day away from work, and some of them were already drifting into the woods for a clandestine church meeting known only to the slaves. It was held too far away for the master to hear their singing and shouting.

Twice in eighteen months, Nat had run away from Briarstone. His back, which had never known a whip until William had bought him a year ago April, was now a tangled spider web of raised scars. He moved with some difficulty because the latest wounds were still painful.

His most successful bid for freedom was when he and Sarah had run through the swamp, pursued by the cruel slave catcher Barley Cobb and his dogs. Nat and Sarah had escaped to Richmond in secret compartments on a farm wagon. Emily rode on the seat beside a local farmer who was a "conductor" on the Underground Railroad.

Nat was roused from his anguished meditations when a girl in her teens caught up with him. "I heard your bell, so you must be Nat."

He glanced at her. She was a mulatto, with light skin like his, and she was pretty. Not as pretty as Sarah, he decided, but she was the best-looking girl he had seen in a long time.

She smiled and fell into step with him. Brown eyes brightening, she asked, "You afraid to talk to me?"

He was surprised that she didn't speak with the usual slave dialect. "No, 'course not," he replied. He glanced around and saw Julius at a distance, watching.

"I'm Delia." The girl motioned toward the woods. "You going to hear Brother Tynes?"

Nat had more pressing matters on his mind than talking to anyone, but he asked politely, "Who?"

Delia glanced around and lowered her voice. "The preacher. Powerful good one, too."

"Cain't be no preacher," Nat replied in dialect.

"You don't need to pretend with me," Delia said. "I heard you talking with George. You both speak properly."

Nat's blood suddenly seemed to thicken in his veins. George was the only slave who knew that Nat was literate and spoke proper English. He stopped and looked down at Delia with suspicious eyes. "When did you overhear us?"

"A while ago, but I won't tell! I wasn't close enough to hear *what* you said, just *how* you said it."

Suppressing a sigh of relief, Nat dropped his dialect. "Where did you learn to speak this way?"

"My first mistress taught me when I worked for her in the big house. Last week another girl and I were sold to Master William here at Briarstone. He said we would both work inside; then he changed his mind. He gave Massie to be Mistress Julie's maid but sent me to the fields." She paused before asking, "What do you mean about Brother Tynes not being a preacher?"

"Because Nat Turner was one, so after they hanged him, a law was passed saying no slave can preach."

"Oh, so that's why our meetings are held deep in the woods at night! I thought it was because the masters didn't like to hear all our singing and clapping. White folks sit so quietly in church they don't seem to have any joy in being there."

Nat found himself enjoying talking to the girl, but that wasn't getting his personal problem solved. He said, "I don't mean to be rude, but I need to be alone."

"Oh." There was disappointment in the word. She added a little stiffly, "I'm sorry I bothered you."

"Don't be offended . . . It's just that I—"

"Never mind!" she broke in. Walking off, she called back, "It would do you good to hear Brother Tynes!"

Nat was sorry she left in a huff, but he continued on, entering the woods away from the other people. His mind returned to his urgent problem. *I've got to run again, and soon,* he reminded himself with firm conviction. *Then I've got to find Amos if I can, and do it all before the speculator comes.*

Nat knew, as all slaves did, that the alternative to running was to work hard with no freedom until death. Most, like George, had accepted this inevitability and did not run. But Nat had to run, even if he died in the attempt.

But how? he asked himself. The only black person allowed off the premises at Briarstone was George. He had been the Lodge family carriage driver for years, so he alone was allowed to drive the master and mistress. He took them to church, to neighbors, or wherever they wanted, then waited with other reinsmen until the white folks were ready to return to their homes.

As Nat continued through the woods, an idea began to form in his mind. *The best way to get started from here would be to somehow get a ride with Uncle George,* Nat reasoned. *But I can't involve him. So how can I work around that?*

The germ of an idea made Nat stop, turn around, and retrace his steps to the carriage house. He found George sitting outside smoking a clay pipe.

"You're back sooner than I expected," the old man said with a smile. He motioned for Nat to turn over a wooden bucket and sit down beside him.

"I just took a walk," Nat explained, seating himself and clamping a hand over the annoying bell to silence it. "I'm feeling better."

"That's good." George puffed on the pipe and blew smoke into the air. "I've been thinking whether or not to tell you something."

"Oh? What about?"

"About the slave speculator who's coming for you. I know him from when I used to drive young Master William's father to Glenbury Plantation where you were born."

"You know the speculator?"

George chuckled. "We never spoke, but I know all about him. He was at Glenbury when your mother was a girl of about fifteen."

"What about my mother?" Nat exclaimed, sensing something vital behind George's words.

He leaned toward Nat and whispered, "The speculator is your father!"

★ ★

AN INCREDIBLE OPPORTUNITY

In sudden shock, Nat exclaimed, "What?"

George replied, "You must know that your light skin came from a white father, don't you?"

Nat nodded, making the tiny bell sound. It was against the law for a slave mother to reveal the name of a white man who had fathered any of her children, but Nat's mother had told him in strictest confidence. Nat also knew Virginia law declared that children born of a black woman followed the condition of the mother. So Nat was a slave even though his father was white.

George reached over and laid a gentle hand on the youth's shoulder. "If I had known it was going to make you look so hurt, I wouldn't have told you about him."

"It's not that," Nat said, trying to recover from his shock. "I never saw him, but I knew his name was Travis. I just never dreamed he could be a speculator."

The old coachman mused, "You must have heard lots of stories about white masters selling their own children born of slave mothers."

"Yes, but it's somehow different knowing that my father could buy and sell his own flesh and blood!"

"Maybe he doesn't know."

Nat blinked. "How could he not know?"

George shrugged. "Hard to say, but it is possible."

That was true, Nat silently admitted. His mother had confided to him that his father was a son of the white overseer at the Whitman Glenbury plantation. At the time, she was barely fifteen and had no choice when the slightly older Travis took her.

A sudden hope made Nat exclaim, "Maybe if he knows who I am, he won't—"

"Whoa!" George interrupted, "I hate to say it, but that's not very likely to happen! I only heard of one or two masters who ever accepted such children as his own."

Nat tried to tell himself that George was wrong, that this time it would be different. But Nat also knew that George heard everything in driving the master to various functions over many years or while talking with other coachmen waiting for their masters. George had heard all the gossip from fellow slaves. He had known Nat's mother when she was a girl. So Nat was positive that George was telling him the truth; it wasn't likely his father would claim him.

"But," Nat said, hope surging again, "maybe this time it'll be different!"

George sadly shook his head without replying.

★ ★ ★ ★ ★

In her bedchamber, Emily fretted over the way Julie had reacted when she wouldn't tell why Gideon had charged into the house that afternoon. Emily slipped a dressing gown over her nightclothes and opened the door to the upstairs hallway. She glanced toward Julie's room just as Massie straightened up quickly from in front of Julie's closed bedroom door. Without looking at Emily, the maid hurried away toward the top of the stairs.

That's the second time today I've seen her doing that, Emily thought. *Why would she . . . ?* Shaking her head, Emily approached her cousin's door. *No, I mustn't think that! Massie couldn't be a spy for the plotters!*

Julie opened her door to Emily's gentle knock, but her face showed she wasn't happy to see her.

Emily asked, "May I come in?"

Shrugging but not speaking, Julie opened the door wide and walked to her bed. She placed a bare foot on the step stool and sat on the edge of the high bed.

"Look," Emily began, approaching her, "you've got to understand that it isn't because I don't want to tell you, but because your brother said not to tell anyone."

"But think of it from my viewpoint!" Julie said sharply. "You went to ask William not to sell Nat down the river. Instead, you admit that you didn't even ask him. Then Gideon rushed into the house and talked to you and William—every servant knows that—but you won't tell me what it was all about, and they don't know!"

Emily deeply regretted having failed to seek mercy for Nat, but Gideon's shocking news had instantly driven the thought from her mind. She said, "Ask your brother."

"I did, and he won't tell me, either! But you can because we're friends! I don't keep secrets from you. Why should you keep one from me?"

"I've told you why, over and over. William—"

"Never mind him!" Julie snapped, her eyes sparking with anger. "Every time I see two servants together since Gideon came, they're whispering. They quit when they see me, but I overheard them mention Gideon running in and talking to you and William alone. I asked the servants why, but they claim they don't know. Maybe they don't, but something's going on. I want to know what it is!"

Emily said evenly, "I didn't come here just now to start this all over again! I've told you what I can. I just don't want us to sleep without resolving this!"

Julie's eyes narrowed thoughtfully. "Did you promise William you wouldn't tell anyone?"

"Well, no, but—"

"Then you can tell me because you're not breaking a promise!" Julie exclaimed triumphantly.

Taking a long, slow breath, Emily explained, "It's the same as a promise. I want to tell you, believe me!"

"But I've got a right to know!" Julie slid off the high bed without using the step stool.

Emily believed that was right, but she had struggled constantly to not antagonize William again. They had already had many spirited disagreements over President Lincoln and slavery. She didn't want to be asked to leave Briarstone as her aunt and William had done once before.

"This isn't getting us anywhere," Emily said. "Can we at least be friends again so we can go to sleep?"

"No! Not unless you tell me."

Sighing, Emily said, "I'm sorry, Julie. Really sorry, but I have no choice." She said good-night and returned to her adjacent bedchamber. She hated having Julie angry with her, and even more so with a slave uprising threatening them all.

★ ★ ★ ★ ★

The coal-oil lamps burned late that night in the Tugwells' small kitchen. Gideon, his mother, and John Fletcher kept their voices down so that the three younger children could not hear in their adjacent bedrooms.

Gideon commented, "William didn't want anyone beyond the five of us to know about this. If we tell anyone else, William will blame me."

His mother said softly, "Our lives and what little property we have is at stake in this. You're big enough now that I don't think he'll ever hit you again."

Gideon wasn't so sure of that, but he recognized that the adults had made a decision. He would honor that.

Fletcher observed, "As master of Briarstone while his father's off in the war, William probably thinks he's doing the right thing. But he's not old enough or had the experience to always make a good decision. Of course, he can do what he wants there. Here we must do what seems right for us. Martha, I suggest we tell the sheriff."

"I agree," she replied. She glanced at the musket leaning against the wall within reach of Fletcher's right hand. She added, "We can't defend this place by ourselves."

Gideon volunteered, "I'll ride in to tell Sheriff Geary first thing in the morning." He was always glad for an excuse to get away from the farm work he detested. He had another reason, too. He would rather write than eat, and he dreamed of someday being an author. In the village, he could deliver a column he had written for the local newspaper. Maybe he could talk about writing with Mrs. Clara Yates, publisher of the *Villager* newspaper, who encouraged him in his writing aspirations.

He believed a good step in that direction would be to get any job on a newspaper in Richmond, the capital of the Confederacy. But that seemed impossible because his father was dead, his older half brother, Isham, was away fighting the Yankees, and Gideon was needed to help Mr. Fletcher on the farm.

"Begging your pardon," Fletcher said, glancing at mother and son, "but I don't think we should wait. It's not safe for Gideon to ride at night with patrollers and possible Yankee cavalry likely to be out. I'll go."

"Tonight, John?" Mama exclaimed.

"Yes. Our lives could depend on it. Gideon can handle the musket if necessary."

Gideon's mouth suddenly went dry with fear, but he didn't want his mother or Fletcher to know how he felt. Gideon looked at the nearly five-foot-long, ten-pound, sixty-nine-caliber smoothbore flintlock, which had belonged to Gideon's late father. Gideon could fire and reload it by himself, although he doubted that Fletcher could handle it with one hand.

"Sure," Gideon said with forced confidence, "I can take care of us if they come."

Fletcher headed out to the barn, where he had living quarters, to get a heavier coat against the night air before saddling the mule to ride into the village. Mama kissed Gideon good-night before he retired to the lean-to that he shared with his younger brother.

Gideon thought somberly, *I sure hope those slaves don't do anything before morning*.

★ ★ ★ ★ ★

Nat shared a bachelor cabin with a dozen other young, unmarried men. Nat awoke to the blast of the cow's horn, which roused field hands from their quarters in the pre-dawn darkness. He had spent a restless night. That was partly because every time he rolled over, soreness from his recent whipping seared his back like fiery coals. Previous lashings had helped him tolerate the pain.

Most of his disturbed rest had been over thinking whether his father would claim him as a son or sell him like a hog. When he slept fitfully, he dreamed about the vicious methods of punishment heaped upon him by Julius, Briarstone's black slave driver. He worked harder and faster than any other field hand, setting the pace which others had to match or face a whipping that night.

Nat, banned from being William's body slave in the big house, was under Julius's direct supervision. He had never forgiven Nat for helping Sarah escape. Nat endured Julius's yelling, cursing, and blows from before dawn until the hands returned to their quarters after dark.

However, Nat realized those weren't the only reasons for his restlessness this morning. He sensed an undercurrent in the slave quarters that was new and strange to him. Before the others dressed and left, slaves named Harry and Tolliver rose from their sleeping pads of corn shucks and slipped outside for whispered conversations. Nat was fascinated by the hint of intrigue, but he had too many problems of his own to dwell on what might be going on.

All his life—from Glenbury Plantation, where he was born, through being sold to William—Nat had been a privileged house servant. While that put him under the master's eyes day and night, seven days a week, it had been far better than what he was now, a common field hand working next to Julius.

Julius's big body suddenly appeared in the cabin door with a lantern. Everyone had gone except Nat. He was in too much pain to dress as quickly as the others had. "You!" Julius cried, holding the light high. "Git dressed an' git to wo'k." He kicked Nat in the ribs.

Nat tried not to cry out, but the pain seemed to have a voice of its own. Through the sudden hot mist that scalded his eyes and the pale yellow light of the lamp, Nat saw the evil grin on the man's unshaven face. He had long ago learned in the big house never to show his true feelings, so Nat kept his composure. As he forced himself to his feet, his tormentor chuckled.

"I sho' wish de massa don' sell y'all. I kin have me a lifetime o' joy workin' y'all to death!"

* *

★ ★ ★ ★ ★

It seemed to Gideon that he had barely gone to bed when the rooster's crowing awakened him. Sighing, he rolled out of his pole bed, grateful that the slave plotters had not struck during the night. His mother was already up and lighting the fire. She said that Fletcher had returned saying the sheriff would soon be here.

It was midmorning when the Tugwells' two coonhounds bawled loudly. Gideon ran out of the barn, where he was repairing the manger, and saw the dogs charging down the rutted lane. An open four-wheeled runabout pulled by a horse approached with Mrs. Yates driving.

She stopped beside him in the lane and looked down with blue eyes behind wire-rimmed glasses. "Morning, Gideon. How are you?"

"Fine, thanks." He wondered if somehow she had heard about his experience with the slave plotters. She had a reputation of knowing all that went on near Church Creek.

Gideon's mother walked out on the porch. "Morning, Clara. What brings you out here so early?"

"I bring great news for your son."

"For me?" Gideon asked, his eyes arching in surprise.

"For you," Mrs. Yates assured him. She reached down to the seat and retrieved her drawstring reticule. "Here." She removed a letter from her handbag and handed it to him, saying, "It's from the *Richmond Sun,* one of the daily newspapers in Richmond. Read it."

Gideon removed the single sheet and skimmed the few lines. Then he blinked in surprise and reread them.

His mother asked, "What's it say?"

"I . . . I'm not quite sure—"

"I am!" Mrs. Yates interrupted cheerfully. "I sent some samples of your columns from the *Villager* to an editor friend there. He likes your work and has an opening for a general all-around boy with potential to learn the editorial side of the newspaper business. He's inviting you to apply for the job on October first!"

Gideon blinked in amazement. "Me?"

"Yes, but there are other applicants, so you'll have to go to Richmond and compete with them. But if you want to become an author as much as you say you do, then this is a chance to learn from professionals and get paid at the same time. Isn't that great?"

"Great!" Gideon exclaimed, turning happily to his mother. But the look on her face instantly reminded him of the slave revolt and him being needed on the farm. "Thanks," he said sadly, "but I can't go."

"Of course you can!" Mrs. Yates exclaimed. "You may never get another chance like this!"

Gideon looked at his mother, who closed her eyes as if in sudden sorrow. Mental agony also seized Gideon because his mother knew how desperately he longed to be a writer. She had always encouraged him in that. But the offer couldn't have come at a more difficult time.

"Thanks, Mrs. Yates," he said, dropping his head so the hot tears forming there wouldn't be seen, "but I just can't!"

DREAMS DIE HARD

Still standing in the yard after Mrs. Yates left, Gideon hadn't hurt this much since his father died.

His mother said, "I know how disappointed you are, but you're young. You'll have plenty more opportunities to learn how to be a writer."

"I know that in my head," Gideon admitted, "but my heart doesn't agree. For a long time, I've ached for a chance to work with someone who can teach me how to write well. That chance has come, and I can't even apply."

He sighed before continuing. "It's not just this slave rebellion situation. You know I hate farming, but this place is all we have, even if it is hard work. Of course, it was worse after Isham went off to war and then Papa died, leaving only little Ben and me do the plowing and planting and things you and the girls couldn't do."

"Hasn't it been easier since John came?"

"Yes, Mama, but with only hand, he can't do what Papa could. And I'm afraid that someday he'll leave us."

Gideon instantly regretted his words as a flicker of pain appeared on his mother's face. When John Fletcher had agreed to stay on at the farm, it was as if she had a new lease on life. She had finally stopped mourning her husband's unexpected death and, to Gideon's delight, had even started singing around the house again.

Gideon quickly added, "I'm sorry, Mama. I shouldn't have said that."

"You spoke the truth," she admitted. "After all, he long ago repaid the obligation he felt was owed us for nursing him back to health."

Gideon thought back to when Fletcher had arrived in the spring and had collapsed with fever. He had brought a message from Isham Tugwell, Gideon's older half brother. Both men had been wounded a year ago July at Manassas.

Gideon told his mother, "Even if he doesn't return to the Shenandoah Valley, until this war is over and Isham comes home, I've got to stay here and take care of you, Ben, Kate, and Lilly."

A small voice seemed to whisper to Gideon, *But don't give up hope about Richmond*. Gideon ignored it as he watched the sheriff turn his horse off the public road and start up the long lane to where mother and son waited.

★ ★ ★ ★ ★

Emily caught William as he stepped out the side door to where a young slave boy held the reins to a saddled horse. "William," Emily said, "please wait a minute."

"I'm in a hurry," he answered.

"I'll make it fast." She took the reins from the boy, adding, "This is confidential."

She caught a trace of annoyance on William's face, but she guessed that he thought she wanted to talk about the uprising. He motioned for the boy to leave.

Emily began, "Julie is very upset with me because she knows that Gideon rushed over here yesterday, yet you won't tell her why, and you won't let me say anything."

"For good reason, if you must know." William's tone was cool. "She might tell our mother, and Mother will take to her bed again. I've got enough troubles without that."

"But I think Julie *should* know."

William scowled and put his left foot in the left stirrup. "Oh, you do? Well, I don't need your opinion!"

His words stung her, but she tilted her chin defiantly as he settled into the saddle. "I think Julie could help in this . . . uh . . . situation."

"The answer is still no. Now, hand me the reins."

Emily ignored that, saying, "I have another request—not for Julie or myself, but for Nat."

"He is no concern of yours!"

"He's a human being, and that makes him my—"

"He's a slave, so he's property!" William roared. "He's like this horse or this plantation; *my* property!"

Emily fought down the angry, defensive words that sprang to her lips and instead said quietly, "I ask your mercy for Nat. Please don't sell him."

"What I do with the servants is none of your business."

"Servants!" The word exploded from Emily's lips. She dropped the reins and stepped close to look up at William. "They're slaves; you just said so! None of these poor people working here are servants!" She instantly regretted her words, but it was too late.

William's voice rose. "We've had this discussion before, and there's no need to go over it again! I'm making an example of Nat! Now, get out of my way!"

He leaned over the horse's neck, clutched the reins, and spurred off, leaving Emily standing in double defeat at the side door.

★ ★ ★ ★ ★

Nat helped finish loading tobacco leaves onto a horse-drawn sled just as Toombs, Briarstone's white overseer, arrived on horseback, whip in hand. He spoke to Julius, who motioned for the sled driver and Nat to take the load to the log-drying barns.

Nat, unused to hard manual labor, especially under Julius's baleful eyes, welcomed a chance to ease his back, which ached from bending over to pick the leaves. He also wanted to speculate more on whether his slave-trader father would recognize him as his son or sell him. Uncertainty gnawed at Nat's heart, affecting his ability to think clearly. *But if he doesn't acknowledge me,* Nat told himself, *I need to think about possibly escaping so he can't sell me into the Deep South. How can I do that with this bell telling everyone where I am every moment?*

Nat stood on the front of the sled beside the black driver until the horse stopped at the open barn door. Nat stepped off, making the bell jangle. The sound caused all the women and girls inside to look at him. He recognized Delia as she tied three of the broadleaf plants onto a stick for drying.

She glanced up, saw him, and thrust her chin up disdainfully. She was obviously still hurt because he had walked away from her so abruptly last night.

He didn't want to her to have a wrong impression of him, so he watched for an opportunity to pass near her in the unloading process. Several minutes went by before he walked close to her. He spoke so softly that only she could hear. "Delia, I didn't meant to hurt your feelings yesterday."

She turned big brown eyes toward him. He thought she was going to smile, but instead, he saw her look beyond him. Her eyes opening wide in fright made him whirl around just as Julius rushed upon him. Nat instinctively ducked, but a hard right hand smashed across his face, knocking him backward, the bell clanging.

"No mo'h, boy!" the slave driver growled through clenched teeth. "Git outta heah and don' never lemme see y'all talkin' to this heah gal!"

Nat staggered but didn't fall. He gingerly touched where the blow had landed. There was no blood, but Nat's ears rang and he expected that his jaw would swell.

Julius yelled, "Now, git!"

Embarrassed at having to take a blow and not defend himself, Nat hurried toward the door but stole a glance back at Delia. Her eyes were still wide, but there was a softness in them he hadn't noticed before.

★ ★ ★ ★ ★

Sheriff Wallace Geary sat silently in the old rocker that had belonged to Gideon's father. When Gideon finished telling about overhearing three slaves plotting a rebellion, he glanced at his mother.

Mrs. Tugwell stood guard at the kitchen window so that her younger children didn't come rushing in. They had opposed being sent to the barn to play after they saw the officer dismounting in the yard. She turned from the window to ask, "So, Sheriff, can you find out who they are and stop them before they carry out their awful plans?"

He fastened appraising gray eyes on her. "I don't have much to go on and no deputies, either, because they're all off fighting the Yankees. I'd be doing that, too, if I wasn't so old they won't take me. But to be safe, I think you and the little children should visit friends far from here."

"No!" Mrs. Tugwell exclaimed. "I will not be run out of our home!"

"I understand how you feel," Geary replied, tugging at the ends of his full, graying mustache. "But I can't be responsible if you don't do as I suggest." He turned to face Gideon and Fletcher. "You two will have to stay to feed the stock and so forth. Is that old muzzle-loader the only weapon you have?"

"Yes, sir," Gideon answered, glancing at the heavy weapon. "It was my papa's."

"Can you shoot, son?" Geary asked.

"Some. But I never shot a person."

"I hope you won't have to. Now, Fletcher, I figure you can handle a pistol with one hand. So I'll loan you a couple, along with a cavalry shotgun."

"Wait!" Mrs. Tugwell interrupted. "We're not a violent family! We don't want to use firearms against anyone, even slaves who're trying to gain their freedom."

The sheriff regarded her in silence as Gideon swallowed hard, thinking how awful it would be to shoot anyone. But he didn't want their house burned or his family hurt in case of an attack. *Or Emily,* he thought.

"Martha," Geary said slowly, "I'm sure Isham and Mr. Fletcher felt the same way until they were caught in a battle. Sometimes there's no other way to protect your life and the lives of those you love."

"I suppose," she replied doubtfully. "I'll try to get someone at church to care for Ben, Kate, and Lilly, but I'm going to stay here to help protect our property."

★ ★

"It may not come to that," Geary replied. "I'll do my best to stop this rebellion before it happens." He rose from the old rocker. "Now, show me around this place, and I'll help plan how to defend it. I'll come back later, and you can show me where you heard those slaves plotting. Maybe they left some sign that will help me figure out who they are. But before that, I'll ride over to Briarstone and see what can be done there."

Gideon exclaimed, "If you do, William will know I told, and he's already mad at me."

The sheriff smiled. "From what I've heard, William picks on you because he was angry with your father for not selling this place to his father. Now that Mr. Lodge is chasing Yankees, William takes his frustration out on you because your mother also refuses to sell this place."

Geary started toward the door. "But William's life and those of his family are also in danger, along with his property. So maybe he'll have the good sense to know you did the right thing in telling me."

Gideon didn't say what he most feared: Even if the rebellion was stopped, William might take revenge on Gideon by forbidding him to ever visit Emily again.

★ ★ ★ ★ ★

The plantation school was closed because the teacher had gone to war, but Emily taught the white overseer's older children under the great oak behind the big house. Young slave children played nearby. Emily knew they were also listening to instructions on reading and doing sums. She looked up as the geese began honking from the front of the house, which was hidden from her view. Hoping the flock was challenging Gideon's arrival, she told the students to keep working and said she would be right back.

She had never seen the sheriff, but the morning sun glinting on his badge identified him to her. She was glad that William was now in the field. Emily walked up as the sheriff dismounted at Briarstone's front door.

"Morning," she said, smiling from under her bonnet. "I'm

Emily Lodge. I live with my aunt Anna and cousins William and Julie."

"Sheriff Wallace Geary," he said, removing his brown hat. He glanced at the Confederate flag flying from one of the white Corinthian pillars flanking the massive door, then back to Emily. "You're that Yankee gal I've heard so much about."

"My family all died in Illinois," she explained.

"I'm sorry, Miss Emily. Is William around?"

Before she could answer, Julie rushed out of the front door and up to where Emily and the sheriff stood. "I knew it!" Julie exclaimed, her face showing alarm. "I knew you'd come, Sheriff Geary!"

"No need to be frightened, Miss Julie," he assured her. "I'll help your brother stop this uprising."

Emily silently groaned, knowing that the officer had innocently been tricked into telling Julie what her brother wouldn't and Emily couldn't. She gave Julie credit for showing no surprise.

"I know you will, Sheriff," Julie replied. "Papa always said he could count on you before you retired, and now you're back working again! What can we do to help?"

"I'm sure William would rather be present before I say anything more, Miss Julie. Would you mind sending a boy to fetch him?"

"No, of course not," Julie replied, giving Emily a triumphant look before lowering her voice. "Sheriff, I'll show you into the library while someone gets William. Emily, I'm sure you won't mind sending for William while I see to our guest's comfort?"

Emily was trapped with no choice. "Of course," she replied, knowing that in the few minutes Julie would have time alone with the sheriff, she would know most of the secret that had been kept from her. William wasn't going to like that—not a bit.

★ ★ ★ ★ ★

Shortly after the sheriff left the Tugwells', Gideon vainly tried to make himself go back to work. Instead, he slipped away to the haymow where he could be alone, leaving his mother to answer all the excited questions from Gideon's younger brother and two sisters.

He peered through a knothole in the barn wall to make sure that his family and John Fletcher were not in sight. Then he retrieved his secret journal from behind a loose two-by-four timber. The pages shared his most private hopes, fears, and dreams. Taking a stub of pencil from the side pocket of his high-waisted trousers, he began writing about what had just happened. He scribbled rapidly for a few minutes, then stopped to silently reread his words.

Even if it weren't for the uprising and the farm work, I know Mama doesn't want me to go. But I'll soon be fourteen, and lots of boys my age are fighting Yankees. I can take care of myself.

Chewing thoughtfully on the end of the pencil, Gideon formed his next thoughts before again writing.

I may not get the job, but at least it's a chance. The Bible says to delight in the Lord and He will give us the desires of our hearts. I want with all my heart to try for that job. But how can I with all these problems, especially the slave uprising?

Gideon turned imploring eyes toward the roof of the barn, but he was trying to see far beyond that. *In less than two weeks, we've got to solve these problems so I can be in Richmond in time for that interview!*

THE NEW ARRIVALS

Gideon hurried into the kitchen where his mother was peeling potatoes. "Mama, I've made up my mind about some things."

She put down the knife and wiped her hands on her apron. "What things?"

"I figure if we can prevent that slave uprising by the end of the month, I can be in Richmond on October first for that job interview."

She looked at him for several seconds without speaking. Then she motioned for him to sit at the table. He slid onto the bench, and she sat across from him.

She said gently, "I well remember what it was like when I was your age and wanted something very, very much. But later I realized that I hadn't always considered all that 'wanting' included."

Gideon had anticipated her unwillingness to support his idea, even though he could tell she was trying to be careful not to hurt his feelings. "I know, Mama. But I've thought this through pretty well."

"How well?" she asked.

"Well, first we have to discover who those slaves were that I heard plotting and stop them from acting."

"That could be very dangerous," she warned. "Besides that, it's really the sheriff's job, not yours."

"But our lives and this place are in danger, Mama, along with Emily and Briarstone! I've got to do what I can to protect all of us."

Gideon's mother sighed softly but didn't answer.

★ ★

"Then," Gideon added, "I'll have to get somebody to help here while I'm gone and find a way to get to Richmond."

"That won't be easy," his mother said. "But if you could, you'd still need some money for food and a place to stay. You're thirteen and have never been away from home by yourself. You'd be alone in a strange city with Yankees trying to capture it. That frightens me!"

Gideon had anticipated she would bring up his age and inexperience, so he was ready with answers. "I'll be fourteen next month. I could borrow a horse or a mule from somebody at church and ride to Richmond in about two days. I could stay with Mrs. Stonum, as Emily did when she was there."

Mrs. Tugwell reminded him, "Emily said that Richmond is so packed with refugees fleeing from the Yankees that nobody had rooms to rent. She was fortunate in being able to share a room with another girl at Mrs. Stonum's. I don't think she had boys there."

Gideon knew his mother was being practical, but he refused to consider defeat on these points. "Thousands of boys my age, or even younger, are fighting in the war. I can take care of myself, eat, and find a place to sleep."

She let that pass without comment. Instead, she asked, "Where would we get a replacement to help around here while you're gone? All the able-bodied men are away fighting the war."

"I don't know yet," he said stubbornly, "but I'll find someone, at least to work here until I get back."

"Suppose you do find someone on a temporary basis, what will you do if you actually get that Richmond job?"

Gideon hadn't thought that far ahead, but he would not give up. "I'll work that out later, Mama."

"I know how much this means to you, but how can you overcome all those difficulties in just two weeks?"

He recognized the wisdom in her question, but his mind was made up and the discussion was making his insides twist with emotion. "I'll find a way, Mama," he said, rising and coming around to kiss her on the cheek. "Somehow, I'll find a way."

★ ★ ★ ★ ★

William had been polite to the sheriff while he was there, but the moment he rode off, William summoned his sister and Emily into the library. He sent Levi out of the room, telling him to take all other servants down the hall until he sent for them. As Emily and Julie entered, William scowled at them from his father's leather chair.

"I'm sure," he began in a cold, disapproving voice, "that you both know why I called you in. Emily, I don't believe you told anyone about this uprising business, but your farm-boy friend told the sheriff against my wishes."

Emily protested, "I don't think he would do that, but maybe his mother did, so he had to do what she said."

"Don't defend him!" William snapped. "Anyway, with every servant on this place seeing Gideon ride in here yesterday all excited and the sheriff showing up today, probably whoever's behind this uprising plan knows why they were here. That'll start every tongue to wagging and make the plotters extra careful."

William turned to his sister. "When I told the sheriff that I didn't want you or our mother to know, he reported how you tricked him into telling."

"It wasn't really a trick," Julie protested. "I—"

"He told me what you said!" William snapped. "I'm surprised because you're usually quiet and mind your own business. Don't start changing on me!"

Emily felt sorry for Julie as she watched her cousin's eyes drop in shame, but Emily's stubborn nature made her do the opposite. "William," she said, looking him straight in the eyes, "now that Julie knows, she and I will join Gideon in trying to find out who's behind this."

"No! You three stay out of this. The sheriff and I will handle it."

"But," Emily protested, "all of our lives are at stake here! We've got to do what we can to stop it!"

William regarded her without speaking for a few seconds. "I don't see how you three can do anything about this, but I guess you can look and listen to what the servants are saying. Just don't get in the sheriff's way, or in mine. Understand?"

Emily and Julie nodded.

"Good." William stood up, indicating the meeting was over. "Now go about your usual routines, but keep your eyes and ears open. Let me know if you learn anything."

Outside the closed library door, Julie said, "I'm frightened. We could all be murdered in our beds, but without knowing who's involved or when they—"

"Shh!" Emily cautioned, looking around.

"Well, we could! Oh, I'd like us to get away from here—someplace where we'd be safe until this is over."

"Your brother won't leave here, and your mother doesn't know about this. So I think you and I will have to stay in spite of the danger here."

"You're right," Julie admitted. "And I owe you an apology for the way I acted when you wouldn't tell me about the uprising."

"Forget it. I have."

"Thanks. But I'm still frightened."

Emily glanced around to make sure that none of the household slaves were within hearing distance. Then she whispered to Julie, "I've got an idea of how we can find out who's behind this."

"You have?"

"Yes. Let's take a walk where nobody can hear us, and I'll tell you. Then we'll talk to Gideon."

"All right, but first give me a hint," Julie begged.

Emily hesitated, then leaned close to her cousin's ear and whispered, "It's about a spy."

★ ★ ★ ★ ★

By the time Nat had returned to the barn with three more loads of tobacco, his jaw was sore where Julius had struck him. Yet that ache was nothing compared to the one that filled his heart.

After careful reflection, he had decided that Uncle George was right: He couldn't count on his white father to recognize him as a son. That meant he would certainly be sold down the river if he didn't escape first. But running a third time wouldn't be easy with the telltale bell hanging over his head. The bell betrayed his every move. The blacksmith had made the contraption, but William had locked it and kept the only key.

So, Nat asked himself, *how can I get this thing off? Even if I had a saw that would cut metal, I couldn't use it without cutting myself. So I'll need the key, but who would dare risk William's anger to get it?*

★ ★ ★ ★ ★

After the sheriff returned to the Tugwells' from Briarstone, Gideon led him to the swamp area where he had overheard the men plotting. Sheriff Geary was not in good physical condition and was soon puffing hard from walking on the spongy peat and sucking mud.

Gideon glanced anxiously at Geary as he wheezed louder and louder and made frequent stops. The boy was concerned for the man's health when they arrived at the small hummock where the slaves had stood, plotting their revolt.

Man and boy searched carefully but found only some human footprints and a few hog tracks. Gideon mused, "Our boar must have made those. I'd sure like to catch him soon. We need the meat to see us through the winter."

"And I'd like to know who made those footprints," the sheriff replied. "But there's not a single clue. . . . What's that?!" he exclaimed, whirling around.

Gideon did the same. Through the underbrush, he glimpsed a black man ducking behind the same gum tree where Gideon had hidden before.

Geary yelled, "You, boy! Come out from there!"

A strongly built black youth slowly stepped out, hands in the air. "It's just me, Sheriff Geary—Dilly!"

"Oh, Dilly!" the sheriff replied. "What're you doing sneaking around out in this swamp?"

"I was following some tracks of a big black boar—"

"That's my hog!" Gideon broke in, aware that the youth spoke without dialect. "He escaped from our farm over there." He motioned in that direction without taking his eyes off the young man, who was about the same age as Gideon's older half brother, Isham. "I was here yesterday looking for him," Gideon explained. "He escaped some time back when the slave catcher Barley Cobb opened the gate to the boar's pen."

"Oh!" Dilly sounded relieved that they weren't going to give him any trouble. He pulled a tobacco pouch from his pocket. "You must have dropped this. I found it where you're standing. I hid when I heard you coming. Thought you might be pattyrollers. They don't always believe I'm a free man."

The sheriff took the drawstring pouch. It had been made of a plain piece of cloth with a roughly shaped heart sewn onto the side. "Dilly, you don't mind if I keep this, do you?"

"No, sir. I don't smoke. You know, that sack looks vaguely familiar, but I can't think why. Now, if you'll excuse me, I'm going back. I didn't know that hog wasn't wild."

Impulsively, Gideon said, "If you do catch him, I'll share the meat with you."

Dilly grinned his appreciation. "Thanks."

Walking back with the sheriff, Gideon commented, "Did he say he was free?"

"Yes. He was the youngest son of one of Mrs. Yates's slaves. You know who she is. She runs the newspaper."

"I know her. I heard she freed all her slaves."

"She did. Dilly's mother and father among them. They recently died of diphtheria. Dilly's now living with another family of freedmen who're farming near the Yateses' place."

Gideon commented, "I thought when I first saw him that he might be one of the plotters, but he's much too young. How old is he, anyway?"

"Eighteen, nineteen—somewhere in there. I've known him all his life. Good family. Mrs. Yates saw that he was educated. He's strong as a bull and has been looking for work, but all he knows is farming."

Gideon looked up at the sheriff with sudden hope.

★ ★ ★ ★ ★

At dusk, Emily and Julie were returning from a stroll down the long lane at Briarstone when a horse and buggy turned off the public road and drew even with them. "Evening, ladies," the well-dressed driver said, lifting his hat with a free hand. "Is William Lodge in?"

"Yes," Julie replied. "He's my brother."

"Oh, Miss Julie! I'm Elmo Travis, the speculator. This is my son, Clement."

Julie introduced Emily and they both curtsied.

Emily saw that the father was in his midthirties, tall, almost handsome, with brown eyes. The son was about sixteen, also fairly tall, slender, equally well dressed, and good-looking, with gray eyes and light blond hair. Emily noticed that Julie seemed uncomfortable as Clement's eyes lingered on her.

"We're early," Mr. Travis said. "I hope your family won't be inconvenienced."

Julie said rather formally, "You'll find my brother in the library."

Julie turned away, rather surprising Emily. But she didn't say anything and walked off with Julie.

As the buggy passed, Julie said under her breath, "Did you see the way that boy leered at me?"

"I didn't think it was really a leer."

"Well, I did! I didn't like him or his father. They have no manners! They're arriving days earlier than expected, and just in time for supper. That's rude."

"There's something about the boy that reminds me of someone," Emily said.

"I noticed that, too. In fact, both of them remind me of someone, but I can't think who."

★ ★ ★ ★ ★

Full darkness had fallen, and all the other field hands had been allowed to return to their cabins before Julius finally permitted Nat to rest. But he was too tired to help make his own bachelor meal or join some in working their small gardens. The master permitted them to grow a few vegetables to augment their sparse diets.

With the hated bell tinkling above his head, Nat approached the carriage house. Outside the large open doors, Uncle George sat on an upturned wooden barrel and smoked his pipe. He looked up as Nat approached.

The old carriage driver said with a smile, "You sound a little like sleigh bells at Christmas."

"Well, it doesn't sound that way to me," Nat replied sourly. He sat down beside George, adding, "I'd sure like to get rid of it."

"That might happen sooner than you think."

Nat ran a finger inside the collar in a vain effort to ease the chafing it caused. "How so?"

"The speculator arrived a while ago."

Nat jerked in surprise, making the bell clatter. "You mean my father?"

When George nodded, Nat groaned inwardly and closed his eyes in sudden anguish. *Now it's too late to run away,* he thought. *Unless maybe tonight? But that bell . . .*

George said softly, "He brought a surprise."

Nat opened his eyes. "What kind of surprise?"

"Maybe you'd better find out for yourself. You willing to risk walking by the kitchen to peek in?"

Everyone at Briarstone knew the kitchen was Aunt Hattie's domain. No slave had more power than a master cook whom owners could trust not to poison them while she created outstanding dishes. Hattie yielded such authority that even white folks didn't dare cross her.

"Why don't you just tell me about this surprise?" Nat asked.

"Because I just saw him enter the kitchen moments before you showed up. The fact that Aunt Hattie hasn't chased him out with a skillet means he's still in there."

"He? My father?"

"I'm not saying. If you want, clamp your hand around that bell and slip over where you can see inside."

Nat's curiosity overcame his weariness. He made his way through the early evening darkness, past the box hedges, and up to the kitchen. It was built away from the main house because of the ever present danger of flames escaping from an open fireplace where food was prepared.

Careful not to get too close to the back window, and with his hand still securely silencing the bell, Nat peered through the glass. Aunt Hattie moved ponderously from the fire with a steaming bowl resting securely between a heavy cloth in her hands. It wasn't until she bent forward to set the dish on the table that Nat saw who else was in the room.

Nat sucked in his breath, staring at an almost mirror image of himself, except with whiter skin. The youth was about Nat's age, same height and build. The stranger had blond hair instead of Nat's curly black locks.

Nat marveled, *We could almost be brothers . . . .* "No!" Nat exclaimed aloud as the truth hit him. "He *is* my brother—my *half* brother!"

PLANNING AND WAITING

The night air was turning sharply cooler when Nat hurried over to George, just as he stood up to go inside the carriage house.

Still in shock over what he had seen in the kitchen, Nat demanded, "Why didn't you tell me?"

George calmly knocked the residue from his pipe into the dirt and used his foot to cover the ashes. "Keep your voice down," he said, lowering his own.

Nat carefully glanced around before saying under his breath, "Well, why didn't you?"

Unperturbed, George replied, "I thought this was the best way to make you understand what I've tried to say so you won't get your hopes up about your father."

"It was like looking in a mirror but seeing myself with whiter skin!" Nat cried bitterly. "I never thought about the possibility of having a half brother."

"There was no point in telling you before," George said, gently laying a hand on Nat's shoulder. "Sit down, and I'll tell you what I know."

Numbly, Nat slumped down as the reinsman explained. "As I told you, I knew your mother at Glenbury Plantation when she was a young teen. She was very pretty, and Elmo Travis, the white overseer's son, took a fancy to her. She had no choice. You were born when she was fifteen."

"But that white boy over there in the kitchen . . ."

"Name's Clement. He was born a few months after you were," George continued. "Shortly after Elmo Travis took your mother,

Lucy, he married the daughter of a well-to-do small planter. Elmo used her money to become a slave trader, and he's done right well. Now he's teaching his son the business."

"Some business! Selling human beings!" Nat exclaimed bitterly. "We have the same father, yet he's free while I'm a slave because his mother has white skin and mine doesn't."

"Not that it's any comfort to you, Nat," George said sympathetically, "but there are thousands of people just like you with a white father and a slave mother. By law, the child follows the mother's race."

Nat jumped up in frustration. "It's not fair! Why should my half brother be free and I have to wear this hated collar?" He struck the bell angrily. "They're planning to sell me down the river where I'll die of fever or overwork in a few years!"

"Watch your voice!" George urged, glancing around.

Nat was so upset he hardly heard George. Grasping at a straw of hope, Nat said, "Maybe when they see me, they'll know who I am, just as I knew instantly who this Clement was. Maybe my father—"

"Stop it!" the old reinsman said softly but sternly. "I thought you had accepted that he almost surely will not give you any sign of recognition."

"I had until I saw this Clement in his fine clothes. Look at me! I'm in slave's rags. He'll always be free and have the best things in life! I live in a shack and will never draw a free breath unless . . ." His voice trailed off as he thought of something. "Unless," he whispered, "you're wrong and my father does admit who I am to him, and he won't sell me."

George shook his gray head. "Even if he did, what do you think Clement will do then?"

Nat hadn't thought of that. It wasn't just his father who could reject him. Clement would almost certainly not acknowledge a slave as his half brother. After a moment's thought, Nat said, "I'm going to keep hoping you're wrong."

"I understand how you feel, but I hope you're not going to do anything rash. Calm down and think about what you'll do if you don't get the response you want."

★ ★

"I've already decided on that. I'll run away again!" Nat strode angrily toward the slave quarters, his bell tinkling rapidly with every step.

★ ★ ★ ★ ★

Gideon's little brother and two sisters had been sent to bed, but their mother didn't want to risk them overhearing what she, Gideon, and John Fletcher needed to discuss. Wearing light jackets, they hung a lantern on the outside of the smokehouse wall thirty feet from the house. The fragrance of smoke-cured ham and bacon blended with the cool night air, which warned of autumn's deepening.

Mrs. Tugwell observed, "The children all sense that something important is going on. I sent them to the barn when the sheriff came with those guns, but Ben told me they watched through the cracks. They'll hate being sent to stay with friends until this is over."

Gideon said, "It's the only safe thing to do until this uprising is stopped. Then we not only save lives and property, but I can still get to Richmond in time."

A slight frown creased his mother's lined face. "I hope you're not going to be terribly disappointed if this mess isn't over by the twenty-eighth."

"It's got to be, Mama! My whole future could depend on that! That's the last possible day I could leave and still reach Richmond in time for that interview."

Mrs. Tugwell sighed but didn't reply.

Fletcher cleared his throat. "Martha, I'd feel a whole lot better if you went away with the children."

In the lantern light, Gideon noticed a small smile touch her lips. "Thank you, John, but I'm staying." There was such finality in her tone that it prohibited protest. She continued, "Based on your military experience, is there anything more we can do to protect ourselves?"

"I was just an eleven-dollars-a-month soldier, but I'm quite sure that we can logically figure out something about these slaves, even without knowing who they are."

"Like what?" Gideon asked.

★ ★ ★ ★ ★

Emily and Julie had donned light shawls against the night air, and they strolled away from the big house to talk without being overheard. They had both been very cautious since Emily had told Julie about again seeing her maid apparently listening outside Julie's bedchamber.

Passing through rows of English box hedges, Julie said in a low voice, "I've been thinking about it, and I just can't believe Massie is spying on me—or us."

"I don't want to think it, either," Emily admitted. "I don't want to accuse her unfairly, but with all our lives at stake, I thought you should know what I saw."

"It's easier to believe since I saw her myself the first time," Julie replied. "As you mentioned, the plotters won't have a key, so they have to depend on someone on the inside to let them in. Yet I hesitate to have her sold just on suspicion."

The sound of a door opening prompted both girls to look toward the kitchen door at the right rear of the big house. Light from inside the kitchen silhouetted Clement as he stepped outside.

"Shh!" Julie hissed, clutching Emily's arm in the darkness. "I'll bet he couldn't even wait for supper, so he got Hattie to give him something to eat."

"Well," Emily admitted, "I'm not pleased to see them because they're going to take Nat to sell into the Deep South, and I can't think of a way to stop it."

Julie waited until Clement entered the house before she said in her normal voice, "I like your idea of asking Nat to try finding out who the plotters are. Yet, as I told you, even if he does and the uprising is stopped, I don't think William will change his mind about selling Nat—not after he ran away two times."

"It's worth a try," Emily insisted. "If the plotters have a spy inside our house, it would help us if we could persuade Nat to do the same for us in the slave quarters. But that could be dangerous for him, so I'm not sure—"

Julie interrupted. "We don't dare approach Nat directly without making other servants suspicious. Yet there isn't much time since the speculator came early."

Emily admitted, "I know. Oh, I hope Gideon can come over tomorrow so we can talk to him about this."

"I just hope we wake up tomorrow."

"Julie!" Emily exclaimed. "Don't even think that!"

"Well, it's true, and you know it!" Julie paused, then added, "I feel sorry for you, Emily. If you hadn't been turned back because of the second battle at Manassas, you'd be safely home in Illinois right now and wouldn't have to go through all this."

"I've given up trying to get back home," Emily said wistfully. "For whatever reason, it seems God wants to keep me here for now, so I have finally accepted that."

"I wouldn't stay if I could get away," Julie declared stoutly. "But with Yankee cavalry riding around plundering everything and then running off, I don't know if we'd be any safer with them than with this revolt. As much as I don't like it, Emily, I guess we'd better go inside and try to be nice to that trader and his son."

The girls turned back in silence as Emily wondered if there was still some way to keep Nat from being taken off by the two new arrivals.

★ ★ ★ ★ ★

John Fletcher finished telling Gideon and his mother what he believed about the unknown slave plotters. He concluded, "Does that make sense?"

"I think so," Mrs. Tugwell replied, "but let me be sure I fully understand. They plan to attack Briarstone first because there are field hands who live there. They work six days a week and only have Sundays off, so that is the day you think they'll attack. Right?"

Fletcher nodded. "Right, and there are only two more Sundays left in this month."

Gideon's heart lurched with sudden hope. "You mean you think they won't do anything until then?"

When Fletcher nodded again, Mrs. Tugwell asked him, "What time do you think they'll attack?"

"At dawn, because it's the one morning of the week when nobody has to be up early. Everyone in the quarters and the house can sleep late except those in on the plot. They would likely strike while everyone's asleep." He hesitated, then continued. "Gideon, judging from what you heard them say in the swamp, they'll assault Briarstone first, then us, then disappear into the swamp. Nat Turner hid in a swamp after his massacre. Those in on our plot probably expect they can hide out there in hopes the Union wins the war and they go free."

For a moment, Gideon thought of what that would mean to Emily and all those in the big house. Suddenly feeling sick, Gideon abruptly turned and walked off.

I can't let that happen! he told himself fiercely. *I sure hope Mr. Fletcher is right and we've got a few days. We've got to somehow find out who those men are and if others are involved. But how?*

★ ★ ★ ★ ★

Nat awoke the next morning on his corn-husk pallet after another night of restless sleep. That was partly due to his mental anguish about his father and half brother selling him into the Deep South. The galling discomfort of the collar and the telltale bell also disturbed his rest. Other single men in the slave cabin responded to the bell by hurling threats and heavy shoes.

There were no clocks in the quarters, and the horn had not blown, but Nat sensed that it was near daylight. He clamped a hand over the annoying bell, slipped into his trousers made of guano bags, then donned his old "Negro cloth" shirt. When new, the heavy, coarse cloth of cotton and hemp would prick every inch of skin, as if made of needles. He pulled on a too-small jacket against the morning chill, carefully walked around other pallets on the floor, and stepped outside.

Nat was surprised to see someone moving between the untidy row of shacks. It was still too dark to be sure, but he thought it was a slender woman carrying a wooden bucket, probably filled with water from the well. That person stopped, set down the bucket, and approached.

"That you, Nat?"

The question was asked in a hoarse whisper, but Nat recognized Delia's voice. "Yes," he whispered back.

She cautiously looked around, then stepped close. "I'm sorry Julius hit you for talking to me."

Nat shrugged. "I'm used to it."

"You must be very brave." Her voice was so low that he had to bend closer to hear. "I heard you ran away twice. The first time, you and a girl went together."

Always mindful of George's admonition to never trust anyone, Nat again shrugged but didn't reply.

Delia asked, "How did you do that?"

"I have to go," he said abruptly, turning away.

"Wait!"

He hesitated, unsure of what to think about her.

"I was wrong to ask that," she confessed. "It's none of my business."

"It's all right." Nat again started to turn away.

"One more question," she said softly. "Are you going to the Saturday night dance?"

The question surprised him. "Hadn't planned on it."

"How about Sunday night church services in the woods? Brother Tynes is preaching with power."

"That's two questions," he replied with a hint of a smile. He added quickly, "I never heard of a slave having any kind of power."

"Then you'll be there?"

He started to shake his head but checked himself, his thoughts whirling. If his father and half brother didn't acknowledge him, Nat had no intention of letting them take him away to a short life of slavery in the Deep South. The easiest way to run away from Briarstone was through the woods and along the river bottom to the swamp. Having done that before, he knew how to reach the Underground Railroad station. Maybe he could even find his brother Amos and they could escape together.

If the hounds don't get me first, he silently reminded himself. *And how am I going to get rid of this bell?*

"Well?" Delia prompted. "Will you be there?"

Cautiously, Nat replied, "I'll try."

"Good!" She gave him a quick smile and hurried off.

★ ★

THE SLAVE TRADER'S SON

The red rooster crowed repeatedly as Gideon sat down on his stool beside the family cow. Fletcher picked up the three-tined pitchfork from where it rested against the barn wall.

Gideon began milking, watching the double streams of milk noisily hit the bottom of the tin bucket. He said, "You know, I hadn't really realized how much work little Ben and the girls do around here until I started writing down all the things you and I'll have to do while they're away. Like feeding the chickens, gathering the eggs—"

"Helping your mother cook, doing the dishes and laundry," Fletcher broke in with a smile. "Personally, I still wish she'd go with them until this thing is over."

"She'd be safer," Gideon admitted as the milk began to deepen and foam formed on the top. "I watched her when the sheriff tried to explain how to shoot the pistols he left for us. I'm not sure she could even fire one if those men broke into our house."

The hired man said, "Your mother is a gentle soul. I'm sorry she has to go through this."

Gideon's acceptance of the fact that his widowed mother would soon have to remarry to survive made him look up at Fletcher. Gideon favored the widower, but so far Fletcher had never indicated any interest in remarrying.

"She's the best woman in the world," Gideon declared. "It'd be a shame if she had to marry that slave catcher."

Fletcher said, "Barley Cobb is certainly no prize."

Gideon waited expectantly, but Fletcher changed the subject.

"You going to see Dilly today and try to get him to help out here for a while?"

"I'll try to see him after I take Mama, Ben, and the girls into town to stay. If he works out, then he can help you when I leave for Richmond."

Fletcher leaned the pitchfork against the barn wall and picked up a curry brush from a box nailed there. "You really have your mind set on that job, don't you?"

"I want it with all my heart," Gideon replied fervently. "At the very least, I have to apply for it."

Running the brush along the big mule's flank, Fletcher said, "I hope you do, Gideon. But you've got a lot of obstacles in the way and not much time."

"I'll do it somehow!" he exclaimed. But a little voice seemed to whisper, *Don't be too sure about that.*

★ ★ ★ ★ ★

Strolling along the English box hedges and past red maple leaves that had fallen to the broad lawn, Emily and Julie paused to look up as a migrating flock of honking Canada geese flew above the trees.

Julie mused, "I wish I were going with them."

"We'll be all right here," Emily assured her.

"At least we woke up this morning," Julie replied sourly. "I wasn't so sure when I went to bed last night."

The girls walked on while Emily mentally formed her next words. "We're good friends," she began, "so do you mind if I say something you may not want to hear?"

"I suppose you don't approve of the way I'm feeling about this uprising danger?"

Emily detected the hard edge to the question and tried to answer carefully. "I'm concerned, too, but I have faith we'll make it through. What I want to mention is that I think you made Massie suspicious a while ago when you wouldn't let her comb your hair, then sent her and Lizzie out of the room." Lizzie had been assigned to be Emily's maid.

"You know why." Julie's tone was defensive. "I saw Massie

snooping around the other day; then you saw her and said she might be a spy. Why wouldn't I send her out of the room while you and I talked about this uprising?"

"I didn't say she was a spy," Emily reminded her cousin in a quiet voice. "I just said we should be careful because whoever's behind this uprising might have a spy inside the house."

"Are you defending Massie?"

Emily didn't like the tension she felt growing between herself and Julie. "No, I'm just trying to be fair to her since we have no proof. What if there is a spy inside, but it's not Massie?"

"Then she shouldn't act suspiciously! She . . ." Julie paused, then said, "Look over there. Is that Nat?"

Emily followed Julie's pointing finger. Nat walked beside the sledge load of tobacco as it neared the barn. Clement moved out of the barn's shadow. He carried a small leather whip as the black driver stepped off the front of the sledge. Nat reached up to begin unloading the leaves, his bell tinkling. Clement suddenly burst into laughter.

Emily asked Julie, "Why is he doing that?"

"Probably because of the bell and collar Nat wears."

Emily's face froze in anger. "I'm going over there!"

"No!" Julie exclaimed. "Don't do it. You'll only make it worse for Nat."

"I'll find a way to distract Clement," Emily declared. She lifted her long hoopskirt above her shoe tops and hurried toward the scene.

★ ★ ★ ★ ★

Nat turned around at the sound of mocking laughter to see his half brother striding toward him.

Clement commented, "I've heard of putting bells on cows, but I never saw one on a slave before. Is that so your ol' black mammy can find you if her little boy gets himself lost?"

As all slaves had to do, Nat hid his feelings and controlled his facial expressions. He also lowered his gaze, because slaves were never permitted to look a white person in the eye. His brimmed slouch hat also helped to conceal his face. Nat didn't reply, hoping his silence would avert further cruel comments by the speculator's son. That didn't work.

"Answer me!" Clement snapped, slapping the light leather whip gently across his open left palm and stepping close to where Nat stood by the horse.

Assuming the dialect he knew was expected, Nat replied submissively, "No, suh. Yes, suh, whateva' young Massa say."

With eyes downcast, Nat could see his own rough clothes made of sacks that formerly held manure. The fine trousers Clement wore marked the white boy as the son of a prosperous father. Clement had not clearly seen Nat's face, but from Nat's brief viewing through the kitchen window last night, he recalled the features so much like his own face. Only Clement's blue eyes and blond hair were different.

"Well, boy," Clement observed, "you won't need that bell much longer. I heard why you wear it, but you've run for the last time. My father and I are going to tie you to the back of our buggy like a dog and lead you off so every slave can see what happens to runaways."

Nat bit his tongue but didn't reply.

"Of course," Clement continued in a mocking tone, "they won't get to see you later when you're standing in water up to your knees, covered with insects away down South in a rice field. You won't mind for long, either, judging from how short a time one of your kind lives with the hard work and the diseases they have down there."

Out of the corner of his eye, Nat caught the flash of a hoopskirt and hurrying feet. Without thinking, he glanced that way as Emily rushed up, trailed by Julie.

★ ★ ★ ★ ★

"Good morning, Clement," Emily said with forced cheerfulness. "We missed you at breakfast."

"Yes," he replied. "My father and I had business to attend to."

Emily was aware that in the shadow of the drying barn, all the female slaves were stealing glances at the scene outside the door.

Yet there was no slacking of their flying fingers tying three leaves of tobacco together.

Clement's gaze moved to Julie. He flashed a broad smile. "Miss Julie, Briarstone's pretty young mistress!" He shifted his eyes to include Emily. "May I be of service to you ladies?"

Emily thought fast, eager to avoid a direct confrontation. "Well," she said demurely, dropping her gaze, "my cousin and I would . . . uh . . . like to know more about how your father . . . operates the business."

"He's taking me in with him as a partner when I'm eighteen," Clement said, sweeping both girls with appreciative glances. "Why don't we take our buggy and go for a little ride while I tell you about it?"

That didn't appeal to Emily at all, but she had distracted Clement from tormenting Nat. She gave Nat the barest glance and saw him sigh with relief.

"A ride sounds fine," Emily said. "Doesn't it, Julie?"

"Fine," she replied dully.

"This way, ladies," Clement said with a broad sweep of his whip hand toward the house. "While you get your bonnets, I'll have a boy bring the buggy around."

He positioned himself between the girls as all began walking toward the house. Emily wanted to glance back at Nat but didn't. She looked up at Clement as he chattered away, obviously trying hard to impress her.

★ ★ ★ ★ ★

Gideon harnessed Hercules while Fletcher was in the house helping his mother get the three younger children ready for the wagon trip into town. Gideon's heart leaped when the two hounds suddenly bellowed and raced past the open barn door toward the swamp.

The revolt's started! They didn't wait until a Sunday morning!

Gideon darted to the door and peered out, forgetting about the sheriff's pistol Fletcher had hidden close at hand in the barn.

"Oh, it's Dilly!" he exclaimed in huge relief. He yelled at the dogs. "No, Rock! Red! No!"

They dropped their tails at the disapproving tone and stopped trying to circle around in back of the freedman. Gideon saw the fright in Dilly's eyes as he stood stock-still, watching the hounds.

"It's all right, Dilly," Gideon called, hurrying up to face the visitor. "Rock! Red! Home!" They reluctantly turned back toward the house, their long ears flapping.

Dilly's eyes shifted to the back porch where the door suddenly opened and Fletcher appeared with one of the other pistols the sheriff had loaned them.

Gideon called, "It's all right, Mr. Fletcher. This is Dilly—the one I told you about."

The hired man stood uncertainly for a moment, then stuck the weapon in his waistband, waved a friendly greeting, and turned around. Mama opened the door, and Gideon caught a brief glimpse of his little brother and sisters peering out from behind her skirts.

Gideon turned back to Dilly, noting the young man's thick neck and well-developed upper torso. "I'm sorry about my dogs," Gideon apologized. "They won't hurt you."

Dilly smiled ruefully. "I'm glad of that. My father used to tell awful stories about dogs and our people."

Gideon led the way into the barn, saying, "I was just getting ready to drive my mother and the others into the village. I planned to look you up on the way home because I had an idea I wanted to discuss with you. But first, what brings you over here?"

Dilly reached up and stroked the mule's long ears. "Nice-looking animal. Big, too."

"Name's Hercules." Gideon bent to hook the mule's trace chain to the singletree. "Couldn't farm this place without him."

With a pat on the animal's neck, Dilly turned to face Gideon. "I keep thinking what you said about splitting the meat with me if I catch your runaway hog."

Gideon had some regrets about having spoken so quickly without checking with his mother, but he knew that she would be fair. He told Dilly, "We'll have no meat for the smokehouse this winter if we don't catch him, so if we get him back, you'll get a proper share."

"That's fair enough." Without being asked, Dilly bent and attached the other trace chain. "I have to get my own place somehow, 'cause the people who took me in already has too many mouths to feed without me around."

"The sheriff told me your folks died. I'm sorry."

"Thanks. Me too." He hesitated, then added, "I also have to find work."

Gideon stood up. "What kind of work?"

"Farming's all I know. Not much call for extra hands among my people, and plantation owners don't like us free blacks around slaves. I guess the sheriff told you we're all freedmen?"

"He told me." Gideon could hardly contain his excitement. "Uh . . . I'm hoping to go to Richmond the end of the month, so we could use an extra hand around here, but . . ." He saw the sudden light of hope flash in the other's eyes and hurriedly added, "But we have no money. We could share our food—my mama's a mighty fine cook—and there's a room in the barn. We fixed it up so's the hired man—he's the one you saw at the door—could sleep there. We could make a place for you. . . ." Gideon let his voice trail off, realizing that he was rushing in his eagerness and not really making the idea very appealing.

"Is that so?" Dilly asked, lifting a massive hand to brush his chin.

"I know it's not much—" Gideon began, but Dilly cut him off.

"Your mama and the hired man go along with this?"

Hardly daring to believe there was a chance to get Dilly on such a weak argument, Gideon could only nod.

"Tell you what," Dilly said. "Let me think on that while we talk about how we can catch that ol' runaway hog."

"Sure thing!" Gideon exclaimed, his voice shooting up in excitement. "Let's sit on the tailgate while you tell me your plan."

★ ★

RECOGNITION AND REJECTION

Dilly's idea for catching the hog excited Gideon so much that he took Dilly into the house and introduced him. After explaining the plan, Gideon said, "Mama, if this works, I thought you'd want to share the meat with him."

She pursed her lips before turning to Fletcher. "John, what do you think?"

"Right now you don't have any winter hog meat in sight, and Gideon and I have been unable to catch that hog. If Dilly's idea doesn't work, none of us will have any of that old boar's meat. Right, Dilly?"

When he nodded without speaking, Mrs. Tugwell said, "All right. You boys can try it."

Gideon happily pushed for his next goal. "Dilly's folks recently died, and he needs a place to live for a while. So while I'm gone to Richmond, maybe he can replace me."

"Gideon," Mama said, "I don't like to remind you about getting your hopes up too high about that trip."

"But it wouldn't hurt to have him help out for a few days right now, just in case. He knows we can't pay him."

She glanced at Dilly. "Is that right?"

"Yes. My folks worked without pay all their lives until they were freed and got their own place. I'll be fine if I get a place to sleep and something to eat."

Gideon's mother turned questioning eyes to the hired man.

"Martha," he said, "if I drive you and the children into town instead of Gideon, we can discuss that on the way back. That is, unless I can talk you into staying with the children where you'll be safe."

Gideon saw a glimmer of interest in his mother's tired face. "We'll talk about that on the ride, John."

"Great!" Gideon smiled. "While you're gone, I'll walk over to Briarstone and talk to Emily."

Mama reminded him, "You've got a lot of work—"

"I'll get it done, Mama," he interrupted. "Besides, I wouldn't be working if I was driving you to the village as we planned, would I?"

She smiled fondly at him. "You boys run along before I change my mind."

★ ★ ★ ★ ★

Clement's horse trotted down the long lane from Briarstone with Emily sitting next to him on the single buggy seat. Julie rode on Emily's right after having pushed past her to get in first. Julie had ignored Clement when he offered his hand for her to enter the vehicle. This forced Emily to sit next to him.

Emily sensed Julie's annoyance by the stiff way she sat, looking straight ahead. Emily regretted causing Julie's distress, but she had done the first thing she could think of to stop Clement from tormenting Nat.

Clement lifted the reins from around the whip socket and boasted, "My father and I are in a good business. Besides his real estate, his personal worth is more than eighty thousand dollars. Most of that's in slaves."

A sensation of revulsion seized Emily. She knew Julie had already decided she didn't like Clement, but this remark made Emily very uncomfortable. "That's a lot of money," she replied.

"I'll be even richer," Clement boasted, unaware of her feelings. "The cotton states need field hands so much that I'll double our business when I become a partner. I can give a two-hundred-dollar diamond engagement ring to the woman I marry."

Emily quickly figured that was about what a Confederate soldier was paid in a year. For that, he risked his life in miserable conditions while this slave trader's son obviously lived in luxury far from the battles. But what really grieved Emily was that Clement and his father's great comfort came as a result of the unpaid labor of some four million slaves like Nat.

Emily glanced at Julie, who tipped her head back slightly and rolled her eyes up in silent demonstration of her disgust with the bragging. Turning back to Clement, Emily asked, "Doesn't it bother you to know those you sell won't ever draw a free breath in their lives?"

Clement guided the horse onto the public road leading toward the Tugwells' farm. "You talk like a Yankee abolitionist."

"I *am* a Yankee!" Emily declared with a feeling of pride. "I'm not an abolitionist, but I approve of them."

He grinned at her. "You're also a saucy one."

The grin aggravated Emily. "I am not one of your Southern women who isn't allowed to have a mind of her own or speak up for what she believes!"

Emily felt Julie jerk beside her. She turned and dropped her voice. "I didn't mean you, Julie."

"Maybe not," Julie replied so softly that Emily had a hard time hearing her, "but I never would have the courage to talk like that, not even to him."

Clement leaned forward to look past Emily to Julie. He asked with a taunting smile, "Don't you know it's not polite to whisper?"

Julie silently turned away, but Emily told him, "I apologized to her for what I said about Southern women."

"I never met a Yankee before," he said. "Are they all like you?"

"We're all different, but I maybe speak out more."

"I like a challenge in a girl," Clement declared. "It's fun, sort of like shaping up a rebellious slave."

Emily's self-control vanished. "That's a terrible thing to say!"

"Don't get angry! I meant it as a compliment!"

"Well, I didn't appreciate it!" With an effort, Emily regained command of her wrath. She needed to find a way to save Nat from being sold down the river. He wouldn't be helped if she annoyed one of the people who was intent on selling him.

"I'm sorry," she said, forcing a contrite smile.

"That's all right," he replied, glancing at her and then back at the road. "Look up ahead. See that white trash boy coming? If I had my way, his kind would be right there in bondage with those . . ."

Emily didn't hear the rest as she recognized Gideon.

★ ★ ★ ★ ★

Most boys enjoyed being with others their same age, but Gideon had always been a loner. He liked to be by himself to think, usually about writing. He always saw things differently from others—the sights, sounds, smells. That's part of what made him want to write. Striding along the dirt road toward Briarstone in the crisp autumn morning, he savored the quietness.

He tried to think how to tell Emily about Fletcher's ideas of when the uprising would be and yet not frighten her too much. He was also anxious to learn if William had made progress in discovering the conspirators' identities.

He was eager to tell Emily that he had already found someone to do his chores while he was in Richmond. Of course, he still had to convince his mother that he was old enough to go by himself, turning fourteen next month. Then there was the problem of how to travel there, money for food and lodging, not to mention what would happen if he got the job, plus the prime necessity to prevent the slave revolt. But at least Dilly had solved one of Gideon's problems. Maybe he could even trap the hog so there would be meat for this winter.

Gideon was roused from his deliberations by the sound of a horse's hooves coming toward him. He looked up to see Emily, Julie, and a stranger approaching in a buggy. Gideon started to smile at Emily, but that vanished when he noticed the young driver.

Gideon stopped as the horse was reined in and Emily called, "Good morning. Where's your mule?"

"Morning, Emily . . . Julie. Mama and Mr. Fletcher drove him into town." Gideon was careful not to indicate the reason in front of a stranger. "I was coming to see you."

The driver commented sarcastically, "Well, she's not home, as you can see."

"Clement!" Emily said reprovingly. "Please!" She didn't offer to introduce the two.

Gideon scowled briefly at the other boy, then shifted his gaze back to Emily. "We need to talk."

"I know," she replied.

Clement snapped, "It's too bad there's no room in this buggy, isn't it?"

"I'll walk with him," Emily declared.

"What?" Clement cried. "No proper young lady walks on a country road without a proper escort."

Julie broke her cold silence. "She has one. Me." She leaned forward to look past Emily and motioned for Clement to step down.

Gideon watched the surprise on Clement's face turn to anger. "No! I will not be a part of having either of you leave this buggy to walk with this . . . this—"

"Don't say it!" Emily broke in sharply. "I told you a few minutes ago, he's a friend of mine."

"Mine too," Julie said. "So let us out."

Gideon saw embarrassment and anger in Clement's eyes. Gideon said, "Please, both of you stay in the buggy. I'll meet you at Briarstone in a few minutes."

Clement's eyes opened wide. He glared down at Gideon, then dropped the reins and reached for the light buggy whip standing upright in its socket.

Emily promptly laid her hand across his. "Please take us home. Now!"

For a tense moment, Gideon observed Emily's and Clement's eyes locked in unblinking conflict. Then Clement released the whip and picked up the reins. "A Southern gentleman always tries to please the ladies."

As the horse turned around, Gideon was sure that Clement would not try to please *him* if they met again.

★ ★ ★ ★ ★

Nat unhitched the horse from the tobacco sledge and led him to the water trough while the driver repaired a harness strap. It had broken just as another load of tobacco was delivered to the drying barn. After a short time, Nat looked up to see Clement returning with the horse and buggy. From the stiff way Emily and Julie sat, Nat sensed that something had happened.

He was even more surprised when Clement didn't stop at the manor house to let the girls off. Instead, Clement guided the horse to a halt beside the water trough.

Clement stepped down from the buggy and said to Nat, "Boy, give my horse a drink, then put him away."

Nat nodded without speaking. The hated collar bell jangled as he dropped the sledge horse's reins. He reached up and took the other horse's bridle, remembering to keep his eyes downcast as was expected. He released the bridle so the horse could extend its neck and drink.

Out of the corner of his eye, Nat saw Clement offer his hand to Emily. She took it and stepped to the ground. Julie followed immediately, ignoring the helping hand. Nat could feel the tension as Julie hurried back toward the house, but Emily lingered.

"I'm sorry, Clement," she said. "I told you that I speak up for what I believe, and sometimes that's not a wise thing to do. I hope you'll forgive me for what I said to you back there when we saw Gideon."

"You're a Yankee," Clement said, "so I shouldn't forgive you, but I will if you'll be nice to me."

"I try to be nice to everyone," Emily replied.

"Then get rid of your farmer friend and let's you and I go for a ride this afternoon—without Julie."

"Oh, thank you, Clement, but I have other plans."

The refusal seemed to jar Clement. He whirled toward Nat. "Why're you standing there? Can't you see that horse is finished drinking? Unhitch him and put him away!"

Without replying, Nat reached up to take the bridle, making the bell tinkle.

"Just a minute, boy!" The angry tone was followed by a hand being thrust under his chin and forced up. "Don't you know to answer when spoken to by a white man?"

"Yassuh," Nat said quickly, using great willpower to keep from meeting the other youth's eyes.

Nat expected to have the hand removed, but it wasn't as Clement studied him. This was such an unexpected and unusual incident that Nat momentarily forgot to never look a white person in the eyes. Nat's brief glance at the other's face caught his surprise and recognition.

He knows! Nat thought. *He sees in me what I saw in him through the kitchen window!* Nat licked his lips, his mouth suddenly dry and his heart leaping. In that moment, he knew that he could either be accepted as the half brother he was or be rejected as just another slave.

"Boy," Clement said, "what's your mother's name?"

Nat swallowed hard before saying, "Lucy, suh."

"Both you and she always been on this plantation?"

"No, suh. We's from Glenbury."

There was a pause; then Clement asked in a quieter tone, "Who's your father?"

"Dunno, suh." That wasn't the truth, but it was the answer expected from a slave who had a white father. Nat was also sure that Clement suddenly knew the truth about their father. He shifted his eyes enough to see that Emily was watching them closely.

There was a long pause before Clement said softly, "I see." He dropped his hand. "Take care of that horse."

The bottom of Nat's world seemed to fall out as his half brother recognized Nat for what they were to each other but rejected the idea. He took Emily's arm and walked away.

In his anguish and disappointment, Nat raised his gaze to look at the couple moving off. He saw Emily turn and look back at him. In that moment, he saw it in her eyes. *She also knows the truth!* Numb over the shock of having his hopes crushed, Nat stumbled as he led the horses away from the water trough. A bitterness he had never known seized his very soul.

It's not fair! he silently raged. *The circumstances of my birth were beyond both my mother's and my control! I'm a slave, as she was. My half brother is free, as is our father. But I will never be free! Never! We're the same blood, so the only difference is the color of our skin! There is no justice for anyone with dark skin!*

Back on Glenbury, before the owner died and the slaves were sold off to different masters to pay the plantation debts, Nat's mother had taught her life's philosophy to him and his three younger brothers and sister: *"Winning is in the mind and not the muscles."*

Nat had always tried to believe and act that way, but as he led the horses across the yard, the cruel rejection by Clement overshadowed that philosophy. He fiercely told himself, *It's enough to make revenge seem right and fair!* The thought frightened him.

ANOTHER BIG DISAPPOINTMENT

The girls left Clement at the house and strolled down the tree-lined lane toward the public road to wait for Gideon. Julie commented, "That buggy ride made me dislike Clement even more than I did before. He was so rude to Gideon! I think Clement only tried to be nice to me because my father owns this big plantation."

The raucous honking of geese announced Gideon's approach. Emily and Julie waved to him when he turned off the public road and headed toward them.

"Clement's not easy to like," Emily admitted. "But I shouldn't have said what I did. That won't help me persuade him and his father not to sell Nat down South."

Julie shrugged. "You know I don't think the same way as you about our servants, so it's hard to understand why you get so concerned about Nat."

Emily didn't reply. She didn't like to keep secrets from a good friend like Julie, but Emily did not dare tell anyone that she had once helped Nat escape on the Underground Railroad.

Julie added, "You remember last night when we saw Clement leave the kitchen, and you said that there was something about him that looked familiar?"

"I remember."

"Well, I know why. When Clement was asking Nat those questions just now, I realized they look enough alike to be brothers, except Clement is white and . . . Oh!" Julie's eyes opened wide in sudden understanding. She stammered, "I hope I'm wrong, but . . . could they really be brothers? I mean, have the same father?"

"That occurred to me," Emily replied thoughtfully.

Julie declared, "How dreadful!"

"I've heard of it happening," Emily mused, "but if it is true, and Mr. Travis knew, would he still sell Nat, his own son?"

Before Julie could answer, Gideon called out a greeting as he approached. He hesitated, looking uncertainly at Julie before saying, "Uh, Emily, I need to talk to you."

★ ★ ★ ★ ★

Back in the field to load the empty sledge with more tobacco, Nat was so engrossed with thoughts of how unfair his life was that he didn't see Julius until he spoke.

"Nat, y'all doin' a right good job," Julius said.

The first kind words the slave driver had ever spoken to him so surprised Nat that he didn't reply.

Julius pointed toward another loaded sledge and two slaves walking beside it on their way to the barn. "See dem?" he asked. Without waiting for a reply he added, "Harry's de driver an' Tolliver he'p him. Y'all he'p dem."

"Yassuh," Nat replied as Julius walked away. Nat stared after him, wondering, *Why is he being nice to me?*

★ ★ ★ ★ ★

After declaring that he must talk to Emily, Gideon glanced at Julie, then back at Emily.

Emily understood his silent question. "It's all right. Julie found out from the sheriff, so William said we can talk with you about the uprising. But we have to stay out of the sheriff's way."

Gideon heaved a big sigh. "That's a relief!"

To keep from being overheard, he and the two girls sauntered across Briarstone's broad lawn, now carpeted with brightly colored autumn leaves. Gideon was anxious to tell them what he and John Fletcher had decided about the slave revolt. However, he waited until he had heard how Julie had tricked the sheriff into telling her about the situation. That gave Gideon an opening for his reason for being here.

"John Fletcher has an idea of when and where those slaves will attack," he began, hoping not to frighten the girls with the information.

They listened without interrupting until he had finished. Julie was visibly distressed, her hands flitting around like butterflies. "That's what William said, too. Our own servants! But we didn't think of dawn on a Sunday! We could all be killed in our beds!"

"We won't let that happen," Emily said firmly, giving Julie a quick hug. "Tell Gideon how we think we can find out who's behind this plot."

"Well," Julie explained, "twice we found Massie, my maid, listening outside our bedchamber doors. We think she might be spying on us to help these men you heard plotting. So we think we should have a spy on our side—somebody like Nat."

"But," Emily quickly added, "that would be dangerous for him if he's discovered."

"Better him than us!" Julie snapped.

Emily sighed. "I can't believe you just said that."

"But it's true!" Julie protested. "He's just a—"

"Don't say it!" Emily broke in, instantly regretting her haste to scold her cousin.

To ease the tension, Gideon said, "It's dangerous for all of us if we don't stop those men before they act. So why don't we let Nat decide whether he'll help us."

The girls exchanged glances before nodding.

"How can we talk to him privately?" Gideon asked.

"We can't," Julie replied, "but William can. All the servants know Nat's going to be sold and that the trader has arrived. If my brother calls Nat in, everyone will think he wants the trader to look Nat over."

Gideon and Emily agreed and suggested that after the sheriff's appearance yesterday, it would now arouse less suspicion if Julie suggested the idea to William.

After Julie left to speak to William, Emily said softly to Gideon, "I sure hope this works."

"So do I," he replied fervently. "So do I."

★ ★ ★ ★ ★

Nat caught up with Harry and Tolliver just as the loaded sledge stopped at the drying barn. They were rough-looking men about thirty years old.

Harry, a big man with a pockmarked face, still held the horses' reins. An ugly *R* for *runaway* had been burned into his left cheek, scarring him. He didn't seem surprised when Nat told him that Julius had ordered him to help.

Harry reached out to the bell attached to the short metal arm fixed to Nat's collar and gave it a flip with his finger. Instead of laughing at the sound as Nat had expected, Harry jerked his chin toward the sledge and ordered, "Unload dis."

"An' be quick," Tolliver, a short, stocky man, added from where he stood beside Harry, "befo' de slave buyer takes y'all off lak a dawg." He rubbed his hands over a stubble of curly black beard and swept Nat from head to toe before saying, "Y'all like bein' chained like dat?"

Nat shook his head, causing the annoying bell to jangle. He was still unable to understand why Julius had ordered him to work with these two men.

Tolliver said, "Me neither. Hate dem chains!"

Neither man made an effort to help as Nat began unloading alone. He realized that Julius must have ordered them to do that, although he couldn't think why.

When the tobacco was off the sledge, Nat rode it with Harry and Tolliver back to the field. They said nothing, but he sensed that they were studying him, watching his every move.

★ ★ ★ ★ ★

Gideon had been eager to tell Emily about the job prospect in Richmond, yet he delayed doing so even after he had reported finding the tobacco pouch, which he had turned over to the sheriff.

"Maybe," Gideon told her, "Nat can help us find out who had a pouch like that."

"That could be hard, because many slaves smoke pipes," Emily replied. "Even some of the women."

"It's all we've got," Gideon said, leaving the broad lawn with Emily beside him. They turned to walk among the English box hedges, marking time until Julie returned.

"What's keeping her?" Emily asked impatiently, glancing toward the house. "It shouldn't take long for William to make a decision about calling Nat in."

"I suppose not." Gideon took a deep breath and told Emily about the Richmond newspaper opportunity and getting Dilly to work for him while he was gone.

Emily stopped and looked up at Gideon with troubled violet eyes. "I know how much you want to be a writer," she said, "but what if you get the job?"

"My mother asked the same thing, and I don't know."

A door slammed and Julie hurried toward them. "My brother is sending Levi to have the overseer order Nat brought into the house," she reported. "William made all the servants leave us before we talked, but I noticed when I left him that they were huddled together."

"That's probably because they know Nat is being sold," Emily guessed, "so they're probably just curious about why the sheriff was here."

"Probably," Julie agreed. "William told me that he had called each of them in privately and offered a small reward if they brought him any information about what others were doing that was suspicious. Nobody has told him anything so far."

Emily asked, "Was Levi there when you spoke with William?"

"No. I asked William to have him sent out of the room. Nobody knows why I wanted to talk to my brother alone. So unless one of them is a spy for those planning the revolt, none of the house servants knows about that."

Emily asked Gideon, "Do you think Nat will help us?"

"I don't know," Gideon confessed. "He has no reason to care what happens to William because he's whipped him and is now selling him. But . . ." Gideon hesitated.

Emily looked at Gideon with understanding. Julie didn't know it, but Emily and Gideon had once helped Nat escape. For that, he might be willing to assist them. Emily said, "But we can hope."

"We certainly can," Gideon replied. "Look! There goes Levi to get Nat."

★ ★

Emily turned to see Levi striding out to the fields, "Oh, I hope he'll help us."

"Me too," Julie replied, "but if he doesn't, then what?"

It was a question that none of them could answer.

★ ★ ★ ★ ★

It felt strange for Nat to reenter the big house accompanied by Levi, who had replaced him as William's body servant. Nat was irritated by the condescending smile on Levi's lips, and he felt especially uncomfortable in his ragged field hand's clothes and the hated collar with a bell alerting everyone that he was present. Levi's smile vanished when they entered the library and William ordered Levi to leave and close the door behind him.

In the brief silence that followed, Nat stood with hat in hand and downcast eyes before the young master seated in his father's big chair. Nat was surprised that the slave speculator was not with William.

"Nat," William began, rising, "I have something very confidential to say to you. If I hear one word of our conversation from any of the other servants, I will whip you to within an inch of your life before selling you."

The threat angered Nat. *He wants something,* he told himself bitterly, *and the reward he offers is a whipping*. It took all of Nat's willpower to keep his irritation from showing in his face.

"I have reason to believe," William said, lowering his voice, "that some of my servants in the quarters are planning an uprising. I will not tolerate that! I want you to find out who they are and let me know. You must do this quickly. Do you understand?"

Nat was tempted to suggest not being sold if he succeeded, or at least the removal of the collar and bell. But he decided it would be unwise to make any request unless he had something to trade.

He forced himself to answer, "Yes, Massa."

"Good. Now, get back to—" William broke off at the sound of a knock on the door. "Who is it?" he demanded irritably.

"Elmo Travis. I saw that slave boy arrive, so I'd like to take a look at him. May I come in?"

"Just a moment, please," William called, then glanced at Nat.

"You find out what I need and fast. Now, be nice to this man because he can make your life miserable if you're not."

Sarcastic words sprang to Nat's lips, but he held them back as William waited for the other man to come in.

Even with his gaze turned down, Nat knew his father was studying him carefully.

William said, "Elmo, you should get a good price for Nat. He's got everything a master could want, except for the bad habit of running away."

"Runaways are worth less. You should know that," the slave trader said to William. Then to Nat he ordered, "Boy, take off your shirt."

"Yessuh, Massa." Nat exposed his back while he watched his father's polished brown boots circle around behind him.

"Thunderation, William!" Elmo exclaimed, "Nobody's going to want to buy him! One look at all those whipping scars and they'll know he's a runner! I should charge you to take him off your hands."

"Don't try driving the price down!" William growled. "I told you why he's earned every one of those stripes. But he never ran away until I bought him in April of sixty-one and brought him here."

"That's curious," Elmo commented, stepping around to where Nat could see the boots again. "Raise your head, boy, so I can check your teeth."

Nat's muscles tensed in rebellion at the thought of having his mouth pried open like a horse being sold. Yet there was no choice. Slowly, he lifted his head but kept his eyes down as the big hands touched his chin.

This was the moment for which Nat had waited. He felt his pulse leap in hope, but he kept his face impassive. For several seconds, Elmo Travis was silent while Nat waited, sensing that his father had recognized a younger version of his own features before him.

Elmo asked quietly, "What plantation did you come from before here?"

"Glenbury, Massa." It was so strange to call his father master that Nat barely breathed, hoping for the slim chance that this moment might bring recognition.

When the trader spoke again, his voice was normal. "William, it's against my better judgment to even try selling a slave with a runaway record like this one."

"Now, wait a minute!" William exploded.

"Hold on," Elmo said quickly. "But if you're willing to take less for him, maybe we can still make a deal."

A scream of anger and disappointment instantly formed in Nat's throat. Rejected by his half brother and their father, Nat threw his head back to let it out. But the fiendish bell jangled, and he checked himself with a mighty effort. He heard William's and Elmo's voices as from a distance, their words unintelligible.

Nat stood with head down, eyes squeezed tightly shut, his heart crushed.

BATTLE LINES FORMED

In all his sixteen years of life, Nat had never experienced such fury and frustration as he did that night. After full darkness had fallen and all the field slaves were finishing their meager meals or sitting outside their cabins smoking and visiting, Nat slipped off alone into the woods to think.

He vented his outrage at his father, half brother, and William by kicking viciously at autumn leaves. Thoughts about revenge clashed with memories of his mother's often-repeated teaching: *"Winning is in the mind and not the muscles."*

He bumped into a fallen log in the darkness, scraping his shins. He sat down and checked to see if the skin was broken. Satisfied that it wasn't, he remained seated. The bell was silent as he summarized his situation.

My own father and half brother not only refuse to acknowledge me, but they're going to sell me unless I run away first. I can't do that with this bell betraying me wherever I go. If I didn't have it, maybe I could look for my brother so we can escape to freedom together.

Nat ignored the night sounds around him while his thoughts flowed one after another. *William wants me to find out who's plotting an uprising in the quarters. But if there is such a conspiracy, and I ask too many questions, my life could be in danger from whoever's behind the plot.*

Nat stiffened at some intrusive ideas: *Could the whisperings outside the cabin at night have any bearing on the uprising? And what was it Delia said about almost getting to work in the big house, but another new slave girl was placed there instead? Also, why did Julius suddenly shift me to working with Harry and Tolliver?*

Nat shook his head, telling himself that there was probably no connection. *But,* his thoughts raced on, *even if there is, why should I help William?*

The silent answer instantly leaped to mind: *Because if there is an uprising, Emily and all the other white people in the big house will be murdered. Maybe Gideon and his family, too.*

Nat rose from the log, ignoring the bell's clatter. He slowly headed back through the woods, knowing that he not only liked Emily and Gideon very much, but he owed them a lot, too. The mental burden was so great Nat wished he had someone with whom he could discuss his problems. Yet he remembered the warning given him by Uncle George when Nat first came to Briarstone: *"Never trust anybody—not even another slave."*

So far, Nat had lived by that admonition. But now he was desperate for counsel. There was only one possible person Nat might trust: Uncle George. But if Nat shared his tormented thoughts with the old coachman, would he betray him? Nat decided to risk finding out.

★ ★ ★ ★ ★

Gideon dried the supper dishes for his mother after she and John Fletcher returned from leaving the three younger children with church friends in the village. John Fletcher carefully checked the weapons loaned by the sheriff when the hounds erupted into deep-throated bawling.

"Someone's coming!" Gideon cried, almost dropping the last dish.

"Martha," the hired man said, "please go into your bedchamber and close the door. Gideon, as soon as she does that, blow out the lamp so we can't be seen."

In the darkened room, Gideon felt Fletcher ease a pistol into his hand. "Careful with that," Fletcher whispered. "I don't think it's the plotters, but we can't take a chance. Get down low and stay there, keeping your eyes on the windows. I'll watch the door. Listen!"

Gideon strained to hear, then whispered, "A horse."

"But no sound of carriage wheels," Fletcher said.

Gideon's ears confirmed that, slightly easing his tension because it limited the possibilities. Patrollers on horseback traveled in small groups, checking for runaway slaves. Sometimes foraging Yankee cavalry rode by together, but never alone. Gideon heard only one horse.

He asked hopefully, "Could it be the sheriff?"

"He's about the only man I know who'd risk riding alone these nights," the hired man replied.

"Hello, the house!" a male voice called. "It's the sheriff! Call off your hounds so I can step down!"

With a grateful sigh of relief, Gideon walked onto the porch and called Rock and Red back while Fletcher relit the lamp. He carried it onto the porch as Mrs. Tugwell caught up with him.

In the pale yellow light of the coal-oil lamp, Sheriff Wallace Geary dismounted and greeted everyone. He announced, "I have a message for Gideon from Clara Yates. I saw her earlier today and told her I was planning on riding out to see you folks."

Gideon was eager to hear the message, but his mother asked, "Sheriff, does she know about the slave uprising?"

"Oh yes," he replied. "She hears about everything, but she agreed not to publish anything until after my investigation is complete and this thing is stopped."

Gideon asked impatiently, "Did she say anything new about my job possibility in Richmond?"

"Nothing new, but she said that if I see you and you decide to go, let her know right away, and she'll send a letter to her friend Mrs. Stonum, who lives there. Even if Mrs. Stonum doesn't have a room to rent, some of her friends might. You know how slow the mail is these days, so let Clara know as soon as possible."

"Tell her I'm going!" Gideon exclaimed.

He heard his mother suck in her breath. "Now, Gideon, I've told you not to get your hopes up—"

"Mama," he pleaded. "I've got to go! Besides, what harm could it do to have her write Mrs. Stonum?"

"None, I suppose. Sheriff, please tell Clara she can write. But how about the slave uprising? Any news?"

"No, not yet, although I've alerted all the nearby white people to let me know if they hear anything."

Gideon's heart sank. "William didn't want anyone else to know."

"He's trying hard to run Briarstone while his father's away, but he's still a boy," the sheriff said firmly. "Besides, he only has to be concerned for his own place and people, but my job is to protect everyone in this county. I think the best way to do that is to alert the right people, show them that tobacco pouch you found, and ask to have anything reported to me that might lead to whoever's behind this plot."

Gideon said, "I understand that, but everyone knows that slaves seem to have a system of gathering news that's as fast as our telegraph. There's no way to keep this uprising secret very long."

Mrs. Tugwell said gently, "Now, Gideon, I'm sure you don't mean to question the sheriff's methods."

"No, Mama, of course not! But if the plotters know that the sheriff is involved, they might call it off."

"Exactly, Gideon!" the officer said, smiling in the lamplight. "Or if they don't call it off, they might postpone it, giving me time to find out who's behind the plans."

Gideon replied, "William will still be mad at me."

"Better that than having the slave plot succeed," the sheriff declared emphatically. "Now, if you good folks will excuse me, I'll be about my business."

★ ★ ★ ★ ★

Desserts were nearly finished after the evening meal at Briarstone. William and Julie's mother had retired to her bedchamber, claiming she was unwell. That left Emily, Julie, and William with the two visitors. A light-skinned slave stood behind each of the five chairs to render any service asked by the white people.

The conversation had gone fairly smoothly until Elmo Travis looked toward the young host at the head of the long dining room table. "William," the slave trader said, "was there ever a more hypocritical man than Lincoln?"

"Don't get me started on that tyrant!" William warned. "Remember his inauguration address? He lied then, and he's still doing it!"

"Do I remember?" Elmo exclaimed. "I memorized his lies from the speech he made." Elmo cleared his throat and spoke solemnly in imitation of the president. " 'I have no purpose, directly or indirectly, to interfere with the institution of slavery, in the states where it now exists. I believe I have no lawful right to do so, and have no inclination to do so.' "

Emily squirmed uneasily in her chair and looked at Julie sitting next to her. Both girls were tense. So far, Emily had kept quiet, her heart filled with anxiety over the pending slave uprising and the revulsion she felt because Nat's father and half brother planned to sell him as if no blood relationship existed. Emily felt strongly that Mr. Travis knew Nat was his son.

Julie, reared in the South, seemed to consider this as normal, so her agitation toward the slave trader and his son sprang from the unwelcome way Clement had looked at her earlier.

William continued, "One of our neighbors who has access to confidential information from Washington this week told me something that really angers me."

Elmo raised an eyebrow. "What's that?"

"Well," William explained, "at a Cabinet meeting on July twenty-second, Lincoln read the first draft of what he called an Emancipation Proclamation. It said all slaves would be free in states he claims are in rebellion against the Union. But William Seward, his secretary of state, suggested he wait until their army had some victory before announcing it."

Clement laughed. "He hasn't had any victories, so he hasn't released it. I hope he never does, either!"

William burst out, "He has no right to say slaves should be free! They're our property, not his!"

Emily had never gotten used to the casual way white people spoke in front of the slaves, as if they were no more than wall furnishings. Lizzie and Massie stood behind her and Julie. Across the table, Emily saw silent male slaves standing behind Mr. Travis and Clement. Levi was behind William. A quick glance at each of the slaves' faces showed they were impassive. Nothing indicated that they had heard themselves referred to as property.

"I agree," Elmo said. "It's Lincoln's two-faced ways that I find offensive. Then just last month, on August the twenty-second, he said something about, 'If I could save the Union without freeing any slaves, I would do it. If I could save it by freeing all the slaves, I would do it. And if I could do it by freeing some and leaving others alone, I would also do that.' "

"That's right, Pa!" Clement agreed. "But remember a year ago last month, his own general, John C. Fremont, issued his own emancipation proclamation in Missouri. Lincoln fired him for it. Now that tyrant plans to do the same thing for all of the Confederacy."

William's voice rose angrily. "This has nothing to do with freeing slaves! It's just another of the Union's ways of depleting Southern manpower reserve in servants and to reinforce the Union cause in Europe."

Elmo added, "Lincoln has another reason, too: to encourage slaves to rise up against their masters."

Emily turned to William and saw that his face had tightened. The visitors obviously had no inkling about the slave revolt now fermenting at Briarstone.

William quickly changed the subject. "When I was in the village this afternoon, I stopped by the telegraph office for the latest news. I heard that our troops under General Lee have established a line west of Antietam Creek in Maryland. General McClellan's Union troops are at a little village called Sharpsburg."

"Sounds as if there's going to be a battle around there," Elmo mused.

Clement dismissed that with a shrugged comment. "There are battles everywhere. Going back to Lincoln, his goal in making that proclamation is only an excuse for his real objective: to destroy slavery. That would ruin our economy and our way of life. I hate that man!"

Emily had bitten her tongue through the various remarks, but that one made her speak up. "You shouldn't say that about someone who's trying to do what he thinks is right to save the Union!"

"Save the Union by destroying the Confederacy?" Clement barked. "I know you're a Yankee, but I can't believe you support that man or such a policy!"

"That man," Emily replied indignantly, "is the president of the United States, and I do support him!"

"Easy!" Julie warned under her breath. "Easy!"

Clement defended himself by snapping, "I suppose the way you see it, you would even support a slave uprising like Nat Turner's?"

"Wait!" William cried, giving both girls a warning glance and then sweeping the five silent slaves before returning his gaze to the young visitor. "Why don't we men continue our conversation in the library? Girls, I think you might like to read in the parlor."

It was more than a suggestion, Emily knew. She was glad for an excuse to end the unpleasant conversation, so she nodded. "Yes, thank you," she replied. "Please excuse us. Come on, Julie."

The girls hurriedly exited the room, but not before Emily glanced back at the five slaves. Their faces still showed nothing. But when Emily looked at Massie, there was a momentary flash of something like anger in her dark eyes. Then she caught Emily's look and quickly dropped her gaze. Emily felt goose bumps erupt on her forearms.

★ ★ ★ ★ ★

As Nat neared the end of the woods on his way to see George, a feminine voice called softly from the darkness.

"Nat, stop, but please don't look toward me!"

There was such urgency in the words that Nat kept his eyes straight ahead. He stopped, his bell falling silent. "Delia?" he whispered.

"Yes. Oh, Nat, I'm so scared!"

The tremor in her voice convinced him that she was telling the truth. He asked, "What about? Where are you?"

"Behind the tree on your left, but you mustn't look at me! They may have followed me here!"

"Who? Why?" The questions came quickly and harshly because

Nat sensed something was seriously upsetting her.

"Three men." Her words were barely audible to Nat, and those that followed rushed out in an urgent stream. "You see, I heard your bell a while ago and tried to follow you because . . . well, just because. But I lost you when the bell stopped. I moved around quietly, trying to find you, when I heard some men talking, real low."

She rushed on, "Oh, Nat! It's so terrible! They're planning to kill all the white people at Briarstone, burn the big house, then do the same to another white family that lives nearby! Nat, you've got to believe me!"

Fearful of a trap, Nat asked cautiously, "Why're you telling me this?"

"Because you know what happened when Nat Turner and his men tried that some years back!"

Nat nodded in the darkness. All slaves had heard about how white folks rose up in terrible fury following the massacre of some fifty other whites. Most of those were women and children. Their avengers not only hanged Turner and his closest conspirators but went on a wild rampage and killed two hundred innocent black people.

Delia asked plaintively, "What should we do?"

WILLIAM'S ACCUSATION

As was customary in many Southern homes, Emily and Julie took turns reading aloud each night in the parlor. Many women considered novel reading and dancing to be sinful, but Julie's absent father had included in his library the works of Washington Irving, Walter Scott, and James Fenimore Cooper, among others, along with writings by all three Brontë sisters.

The girls were well into Emily Brontë's *Wuthering Heights*, but after the controversy at dinner, Emily was so distressed she opened the book but didn't read.

"Clement really upset me!" she exclaimed. "I can't imagine why he would even suggest that my supporting President Lincoln would make me support a slave uprising!"

"I tried to warn you," Julie replied, "but it was too late. William practically threw us out just now."

"It seems to me," Emily said angrily, "that he thinks it's important to be nice to those slave people so they'll pay him a good price for Nat."

"You shouldn't be too hard on him, Emily. He has a man's responsibility in Papa's absence, and that's a heavy load. Especially when he knows there's a planned uprising of some of our servants."

"I know," Emily admitted, calming down a little. "It's bad enough for you and me to know that someone is planning to kill all of us and yet not know who's involved so it can be prevented."

Julie replied, "What makes this so frightening is that the South has four million slaves who could revolt against five million whites. That includes able-bodied men who are off fighting the Yankees. Only women, children, old men, and some young men remain home."

Emily tried to assure her cousin. "I've read some of the books in William's library. There hasn't been an organized slave uprising in about thirty years—not since Nat Turner tried it here in Virginia."

"There were others before that," Julie said. "I've heard about them off and on all my life."

"I've read their names," Emily replied. "There was the Stono Rebellion in the 1700s, Gabriel Prosser in 1800, and Denmark Vesey in 1822. None succeeded. There were some female blacks involved in a few of those uprisings. I don't remember their names, though." She silently added, *I hope Massie, your maid, isn't involved in this one.*

Emily recalled the bloody aftermath of Nat Turner's rebellion in 1831, and goose bumps formed on the back of her neck. Of fifty-five white people massacred, eighteen had been women. Twenty-four were children. Avenging whites killed upwards of two hundred blacks. Of those, most were innocent of any connection to the revolt. Emily admitted, "It's depressing, but I have faith this one will be stopped before it happens."

"Maybe," Julie said hopefully, "one of my brother's offers to the servants for information about anything suspicious will soon pay off. If not, we could all be . . ." She shuddered and fell silent.

"Don't be discouraged," Emily replied. "Let's keep praying and doing all we can to solve this thing. Maybe Nat will decide to help us."

"Gideon doesn't think so," Julie reminded her. "He was right in saying that Nat has no reason to care what happens. Not after William whipped him twice and is now selling him."

Emily said confidently, "I still believe that something will convince him to help us. Now, let's think about what we can do to find out who's behind this."

★ ★ ★ ★ ★

In the carriage house with its smells of leather and horses, Nat sat beside George on the single seat of an open four-wheeled runabout. In hushed tones, Nat told about William ordering him to spy on others in the slave quarters and what Delia had overheard from three men plotting in the woods.

Nat concluded, "I've always had to make my own decisions, but I'm so emotionally involved in this situation that I don't know what to do. You're the only one I can talk with."

George took an unlit pipe from his mouth. William strictly prohibited any fire around the ornate town coach, the light buggy, the runabout, the leather harness, and other equipment hanging on the walls. "Nat, do you remember when you first came here and I told you never to trust anybody?"

"Yes. You said to not even trust another slave."

"Then how do you know you can trust me?"

Nat shrugged. "Just a feeling, I guess, and I have to take the chance. Besides, you've been here for years, and you also know what goes on at every plantation around here. If anyone had heard anything, you'd know about it."

George thoughtfully sucked on the empty pipe before speaking. "I don't know who's behind this rebellion, but I could make some pretty good guesses. So where do you want me to start?"

"With reasons or motive," Nat promptly replied. "After I left Delia, I thought that the first thing to consider is why anyone would do such a terrible thing."

"Almost every slave on this place has a reason to hate the master. Besides not being free, most have been whipped or severely punished, many more than once, like you. Yet most of us have never tried to run away, and most of us wouldn't hurt the master or his family."

Nat suppressed a groan. "That's not much help."

"No, I suppose not," George agreed. "But if we could figure out not only who has a strong motive but also has hatred or bitterness toward the master, that might help."

"Do you know who feels that way?"

"I have some pretty good ideas, even though we're taught to hide our emotions—especially from white folks. But I've lived a long time and noticed things that others may not."

"Such as?"

George got down from the runabout, moving stiffly because of aging bones and muscles. He checked the single window and the door before returning to his seat. "Can't be too careful," he commented.

Nat prompted impatiently, "Well?"

"I saw you, Harry, and Tolliver bringing sledge loads of tobacco into the drying barn."

Nat saw no relevance to that and his question, so he said a little testily, "Julius told me to do that."

"Did you notice the scar on Harry's face?"

"Yes. The letter *R* had been burned into it."

"Stands for 'runaway.' William's father did that to Harry a few years back. So it's a good thing the old master was off chasing Yankees when you ran, or your face might look like that, too."

Nat controlled his impatience, hoping that George was going somewhere with this.

George continued in a low tone, "Tolliver's scars can't be seen because they're inside from when William's father sold his two little boys."

Nat's insides suddenly churned as he recalled the heartbreak he had felt when his own mother and siblings had been sold off a couple of years before.

George continued, "Tolliver begged with tears for the old master to not do it, but the master said he didn't need any more little pickaninnies. Their mother never got over it and sort of died inside before she actually died. For a while, I thought the same thing would happen to Tolliver."

Nat's agitated insides lurched again before he asked, "What about Julius? Since I was brought back and put to work under him, he's hit me and generally treated me like dirt. He blames me because a slave girl he liked escaped with me the first time."

"Julius is hard on everyone," George replied. "It's a slave driver's job to set a fast pace that others must match to keep up or be punished."

"Until today, he made me work right beside him so that I was never out of his reach. He even hit me in front of the women at the drying barn. Today he surprised me by saying something nice and sending me to work with Harry and Tolliver. I can't figure that out."

"You have to know more about him to understand him," George said thoughtfully. "For instance, did you know he once saved the old master's life?"

Gideon's eyebrows shot up in surprise. "Really?"

George nodded. "It was in the winter about five or six years ago. We had a very hard freeze. The old master fell through the ice on the river. A half dozen slaves were nearby, but only Julius tried to help the master. Julius couldn't swim, but he crawled on his belly across the ice with a limb and pulled the master to safety. Master didn't even get sick, but Julius caught cold and nearly died. His wife nursed him back to health."

"His wife?" Nat asked in surprise. "He planned to marry Sarah before she and I ran away together."

"I'll explain that in a minute," George replied. "But first you should know that the old master sold the other slaves who'd stood by while he nearly drowned. He told Julius that he would be free in one year. Of course, that never happened. After two years, Julius made the mistake of mentioning it to the old master. He denied ever saying it. Well, Julius turned into the slowest worker in the fields. A few months later, the old master suddenly sold Julius's wife and four children."

George shook his head. "Some time later, when I was waiting for the master at another plantation, I learned that all four of Julius's children died of smallpox. Their mother died of a broken heart."

Nat could understand why Julius wanted revenge, but Nat could not approve of murder.

George continued, "Well, you wouldn't believe the change in Julius. Instead of working even slower, he worked so fast that the old master made him the driver."

Nat commented, "You'd think that he would have run away, or at least tried to, instead of becoming the fastest worker in the fields."

George thoughtfully rubbed the pipe bowl between his palms. "That's one way of looking at it."

There was something about the way he said it that made Nat look sharply at him. "What other way is there?"

The old driver stretched without replying. After a big yawn, he said, "It's getting late. An old man needs his sleep. I hope you understand."

Nat frowned, surprised at being dismissed so unexpectedly. He met George's eyes and saw something there that made him exclaim softly, "I think I do!"

★ ★ ★ ★ ★

For the next two days, Gideon was busy teaching Dilly how to do his chores and other farm work. The boys also squeezed out time to make a homemade trap of tree limbs and placed it on the sledge before hauling it to the swamp.

The Tugwells' two hounds sniffed the cage-like structure while Gideon said truthfully, "Dilly, you do good work." He eyed the four-inch gaps between the side poles. "That'll hold the boar if he'll enter it."

Dilly flashed a pleased smile but didn't speak as he backed the mule into position in front of the sledge.

Gideon gave the sturdy poles a couple of hard pats, then glanced at the only opening at the rear. An ear of corn was suspended inside, near the closed front end. If the escaped hog entered and took hold of the bait, the heavy suspended door would instantly drop, trapping him.

"Dilly," Gideon added, "if this works the way you say it will, we'll all have good eating this—"

He broke off as the hounds suddenly whirled around, bawled loudly, then raced across the yard with flapping ears. A young rider on a lathered horse had just turned off the public road from the village and galloped up the long lane toward them.

"That's Edwin Toombs!" Gideon cried, fearful that the son of the white overseer at Briarstone was bringing bad news about the uprising. Edwin was three years older than Gideon, who ran to meet him.

Edwin yanked the horse to a stop, shouting, "I'm on my way home to Briarstone, but I thought you'd like to hear the latest war news! There was a terrible big battle yesterday in Maryland!" His crooked teeth showed as he added breathlessly, "General Lee and McClellan fought at a place called Antietam Creek near Sharpsburg. Awful casualties! Lee is pulling out of Maryland today!"

Knowing his older half brother was in General Lee's army, Gideon asked anxiously, "How do you know this?"

"I was in the village when the wire reports came in." Edwin removed his slouch hat and wiped a dirty sleeve across his forehead. He began to turn his mount around. "Well, gotta get to Briarstone with the news."

"Wait! Who won?"

"Nobody knows yet. But so far more men have been killed, wounded, or missing than any battle of the war! One report claimed thirteen thousand casualties but another said nearly forty thousand on both sides. That's all I heard. Now I've got to get . . ." He left the sentence dangling and glanced beyond Gideon. "You got yourself a slave boy?"

"That's Dilly," Gideon explained. "A freedman. He works here now."

"You ain't working with him, are you?"

"Yes. He's a good . . ." Gideon stopped, sensing Edwin's disapproval.

Edwin frowned down from the saddle at Gideon. "Just 'cause you and me are poor don't mean we ain't too proud to work beside the likes of him."

Through long discussions with Emily, Gideon had changed his mind about slavery being natural and had even befriended Nat and Dilly. But he wasn't quite prepared for the challenges he would face for his new stand. He could imagine the jeers of other boys in the village and maybe even sneers of adults. He wanted to explain that his future might depend on Dilly, but he hesitated.

Edwin seemed to accept Gideon's silence as meaning he was friends with the freeman. Slapping his hat back on, Edwin declared, "Just wait till everybody hears about this!" He spun the lathered horse around and galloped down the lane.

Gideon groaned quietly in tortured awareness that he had failed to stand up and say what he believed. What if Dilly had overheard? Would he be hurt and offended at Gideon, maybe even quit? Taking a deep breath, Gideon slowly turned around to look at Dilly.

★ ★ ★ ★ ★

Something was up. Emily knew it when she and Julie entered the library at William's invitation relayed through Levi.

From his father's big chair, William told the girls to take seats. Turning to his body servant, he said, "Levi, leave us, and close the door behind you."

Both girls exchanged glances as Levi obeyed and William shifted his eyes back to his cousin and sister. He grinned with satisfaction. "Every servant in this house has turned into an informer since I privately offered a reward for information about anything unusual."

"You've learned who's behind the uprising?" Emily asked eagerly.

"Not yet, but for a few pieces of colored ribbon and some other worthless trinkets, I was told who's been acting suspiciously."

"It's Massie!" Julie exclaimed breathlessly. "Both Emily and I saw her listening outside our bedchamber doors a few days ago."

William nodded. "I heard about that from two other servants. When I called Massie in to ask about it, she insisted she was just bending over to pick up something. She seemed very sincere."

Emily didn't say anything, but thought that anyone who was twice caught eavesdropping should still be under suspicion.

"If not Massie, then who?" Julie cried.

William replied grimly, "That should be obvious: Nat!"

CRUEL WORDS

Emily stared in disbelief at William. "You think Nat is behind this uprising?"

"He's the most logical suspect," William explained, glancing from Emily to Julie and back to Emily. "In the time he worked as my personal servant, I saw that he's very bright. Probably the brightest of all the servants, household and field."

"But," Emily protested, "that's no reason to suspect him of such a terrible plan!"

"That's not the only reason," William snapped, his eyes challenging Emily. "He has courage; otherwise, he would not have run away twice. Now he knows that the speculator is already here to sell him down the river. That's enough reason to make him want revenge."

"I don't believe Nat would do that!" Emily declared stoutly. She turned to Julie. "Can you?"

Julie dropped her eyes without answering, but Emily would not abandon her convictions. "William," Emily said firmly, turning back to face him, "I absolutely don't believe Nat is involved in this!"

He stood abruptly, sudden fury brightening his eyes. "Well, I do!" he cried. "That's all that counts because I'm the master at Briarstone while my father is away! Now, stop arguing with me!"

"I'm not arguing! I'm simply saying that you have one belief, I have another. I'm sure I'm right!"

William glared at her. "You are the most stubborn person I

know! But are you so sure you're right that you'd care to make a wager?"

"I don't bet."

"In other words, you're admitting that you don't believe strongly enough to wager on it?"

Stung, Emily cried, "I *do* believe it, but I have nothing to wager—no money, nothing!"

"Then why do you stick up for Nat?"

Emily dared not say that she had helped him escape the first time, and that was because she trusted him and thought he deserved to be free.

"Because," she replied, "I believe that he, and all slaves, should be free. So here's what I'll do: If Nat is innocent, you not only change your mind about selling him to that man and his son, but you restore him to service in this house."

Raising his eyebrows, William mused, "You really are impudent, but what if I'm right and you're wrong?"

Realizing she had trapped herself, Emily hesitated, her mind flailing about for a logical answer. "Then," she said, taking a deep breath and wondering if she was being foolish, "I'll promise to never again voice my Union opinions in the presence of your guests."

William surprised her by grabbing her right hand and giving it a shake. "You've got a deal!"

Julie poked Emily in the ribs and whispered, "Now you've done it!"

★ ★ ★ ★ ★

In the late afternoon, Gideon and Dilly were repairing a snake fence by the public road when Edwin Toombs and a friend about the same age approached on horseback.

"Well, Johnny," Edwin said sneeringly as their two horses came even with the young farmer, "didn't I tell you? No pride at all—working right beside one of them, same as if they was both Negroes instead of one of each."

Gideon heard Dilly suddenly suck in his breath as though he knew what was coming. He whispered to Dilly, "It'll be all right."

Gideon turned to face the two tormentors as they stopped their mounts. "Dilly works for us," Gideon said, "same as John Fletcher."

"It ain't the same," Edwin shot back, "because Fletcher fought the Yankees!"

The one called Johnny shifted his corpulent body in the saddle and stroked a scraggly blond mustache. "Gideon, you shame all us white people by working with a slave."

"He's no slave," Gideon replied sharply. "He's a freedman."

"So?" Johnny challenged. "He's still a Negro."

Gideon searched for a reply that could quickly end the discussion. "What counts is that he's a good person, not one who goes riding around heckling someone making an honest living. Now, he and I have work to do, so why don't you two just ride on and leave us alone?"

Edwin drew back in the saddle, apparently surprised at Gideon's resistance, but Johnny leaned down and sneered, "We'll go when we're ready. Fact is, maybe we'll first step down and teach you a lesson."

Gideon heard Dilly's hammer drop into the dirt just before he stepped forward to stand beside him. Spreading his legs to brace himself, Dilly clenched big fists but said nothing.

Johnny hesitated, studying the strongly built black youth before asking, "Boy, you ain't willing to hit a white man, are you? Knowin' what'll happen to you?"

Dilly said softly with a faint hint of a smile, "I just squash bugs and stomp on snakes."

Johnny stiffened in the saddle, and his face contorted in rage at the insult. But he hesitated, his eyes again sweeping Dilly's powerful build.

"Let it go, Johnny," Edwin urged. "Let's get out of here." He dug heels into his horse's flanks.

For a moment longer, Johnny hesitated, the fire going out of his eyes. He wordlessly followed his friend.

Gideon and Dilly grinned at each other before Dilly said, "Thanks."

"You're welcome." Gideon bent to retrieve Dilly's hammer and handed it back to him.

Dilly nodded as he took it. "Seeing those two reminded me why that tobacco pouch I found in the swamp looked familiar."

Gideon blinked his surprise and asked, "Why's that?"

Dilly explained, "A few years ago, I went with my father, who was hired as a freedman, to shoe some horses at Briarstone when their slave farrier took sick. I wandered off and saw an old mammy, too broken down to work the fields anymore, making a tobacco pouch with a heart-shaped decoration."

Gideon exclaimed, "You mean the same pouch—"

"I'm quite sure it is," Dilly interrupted. The reason I remember is because the rider just now—the one called Edwin—tried to get her to give it to him, but she wouldn't because she said it was for a friend."

Gideon's face lit up with hope. "What was the woman's name? Who'd she make it for?"

Shrugging, Dilly admitted, "I don't know."

"Maybe what you do remember will help the sheriff," Gideon replied. "We'll have to tell him."

"She could have been sold by now, or even died."

"I know, " Gideon said, "but—" He checked himself, realizing he had almost mentioned that telling the sheriff might help stop the uprising. "But thanks for telling me, Dilly." Gideon didn't explain, but he knew he would have to pass that information on to Sheriff Geary as soon as possible.

★ ★ ★ ★ ★

Through the shortening autumn afternoon, Nat continued to work with Harry and Tolliver. He again knew they were studying him. When they weren't looking at him, he studied them. When Nat could, he also followed Julius with his eyes. There was nothing suspicious about any of their actions, but Nat believed what the old reinsman had said about each man's tragedy. Nat thought he understood that George had implied much more, but he couldn't be sure. Somehow, he had to learn more.

It was dusk when the last load of harvested tobacco had been brought to the log-drying barns and the team put away. Julius strode purposefully toward the three men. "Nat, y'all kin talk to dat Delia gal anytime." Without waiting for a reply, the slave driver turned and walked away.

There was still enough light that Nat could see both Harry and Tolliver grinning at him. He wasn't sure what was going on, but Nat was greatly relieved. None of the three spoke as they made their way to the horse-watering trough to wash up.

Field hands traditionally worked from shortly after dawn until darkness except Sundays, and everyone was usually exhausted at nightfall. It didn't surprise Nat that neither Harry nor Tolliver spoke. Nat didn't try to engage them in conversation because he had vainly done that throughout the day.

Harry dried his scarred face on an old sack and walked off toward the slave quarters. Tolliver noisily jerked his head from where he had plunged it into the water. His short, thickset body was barely visible against the fading skyline.

He shook his head vigorously, spraying droplets on Nat. Tolliver reached over and flipped the collar bell as he had done before. "Sho' glad I don' hab dat on me!"

Sensing an opportunity to draw Tolliver out, Nat agreed. "I don't lak it none, dat's fo' sho'."

"You lak hoecake?" Tolliver asked, reaching for the sack towel.

"Ain't nothin' so fine to eat," Nat replied.

"Den hab suppa wid me an' a neighbor lady dat make me hoecake mos' ever' night, fresh outa de ashes." He leaned over and lowered his voice. "Sometimes dis Delia come wid dat lady."

Nat realized it might be a trap, but there was too much at stake to turn this down. He nodded. "What time?"

★ ★ ★ ★ ★

Emily perched on the edge of Julie's high bed and watched her wash up in the ceramic basin on the white marble-topped stand. "What have I done?" Emily repeated what she had so often asked since meeting with William.

The girls had dismissed both maids because of the concern about a possible spy among the house servants. Julie turned with a wet washcloth in her hands. She said good-naturedly, "If you lose, you're likely going to nearly burst every time anybody says something against Lincoln or in favor of slavery, but you can't answer."

"I know." Emily suppressed a groan, then quickly tried to be positive. "But I don't expect to lose. Although I suppose if I did, it could be the Lord's way of chastising me for falling into wagering."

"You get most of your prayers answered, it seems to me," Julie declared. "Well, except for getting back to Illinois. Every time you think you're on your way, boom! You're stopped and back here again."

"We all have trials of our faith," Emily said. "I guess I'm tested so much because I long so very much to see my friend Jessie."

"Are you sure it's just Jessie you want to see so much, and not her brother?"

Even though there was a teasing tone in Julie's question, Emily strongly protested. "No, of course not! Brice is not only Jessie's big brother, but he's like one to me, too."

"Well, it's obvious that he doesn't think of you as just a sister. Twice he's said he's going to someday marry you."

Emily felt a flush touch her cheeks at the truth of that statement. She tried to shift the subject. "Brice is like Gideon: both friends. Nothing more."

"You're going to be fourteen in less than three months, so don't tell me you haven't been thinking about both of them as beaus!"

Sliding off the bed, Emily hurried across the room and looked into the vanity mirror. There was a hint of pink on her cheeks. "I don't want to talk about it," she said firmly. Pausing, she added, "As I told your brother, I absolutely don't believe Nat is involved in this uprising situation!"

Julie wrung her washcloth out over the basin and hung it on the rack to dry. "I can take a hint," she said. "No more talk about beaus. But as for your faith in Nat, you don't have much time to prove you're right. Mr. Travis and Clement will have him out of here real fast unless Nat's innocence can be proved first."

"I know." Emily turned from the mirror to face her cousin. "I really feel sorry for slaves, and I'm in favor of them all being free, as is President Lincoln. But I don't think slaves rebelling to kill and burn is right, either. Do you realize how fast the time is passing?"

"Don't say it!" Julie exclaimed. "I get nightmares the way it is! I probably won't sleep a wink Saturday night, knowing what may happen Sunday morning."

A tingle of fear rippled over Emily's body. She wondered, *Why hasn't Nat sent word to William about what he told him to do?* She tried to shake the thought away, but another popped up in its place. *Could I possibly be wrong about Nat?*

★ ★ ★ ★ ★

Gideon and Dilly checked the homemade hog trap, which they had placed at the edge of the swamp and baited with two ears of corn. Disappointed but not surprised that it was empty, they rode the sledge back to the barn, where Mrs. Yates was just stopping in her buggy.

Gideon called off the bawling hounds and hurried to meet her while Dilly unhitched the mule.

"I can't stay, Gideon," she called, reaching down to the floorboards and picking up some books. "I brought you some good reading material. All good writers are readers. Also, how are plans for Richmond coming along?"

"Not very well, I'm afraid," he confessed, reaching to take the books. "So far, all I've got is Dilly to replace me when I do go."

The bright blue eyes lit up. "I notice you said 'when' not 'if' you go."

"I'm still praying and hoping," he said, hearing the door open behind him and his mother's footsteps on the porch. "And I'm doing everything I know how to help make those prayers get answered."

"Good!" Mrs. Yates waved and raised her voice. "I can't stay, Martha. I just brought some books for your son and to bring some good news."

Mother and son asked together, "What good news?"

"The sheriff told me about the slave situation, and he said he's making progress. That's all he revealed, but I thought you'd like to know." She picked up the reins and clucked to the horse. "Sorry I can't stay longer. Oh, I almost forgot: The sheriff tells me that some Union cavalry patrols have been seen in this area. Might keep an eye out for them." She turned the animal around and headed back down the long lane with the hounds baying behind her.

"I wonder what kind of progress?" Gideon asked, turning to his mother.

"I wish I knew," she said with a sigh. "Sunday morning is just three days away."

★ ★ ★ ★ ★

Tolliver had said supper would be at nine, so shortly before then, Nat left the cabin he shared with other unmarried men. As he made his way through the dark, he was surprised to see a white face in the pale yellow light of a coal-oil lamp that shone from a partly open cabin door.

Nat dropped his eyes, as was expected when a slave met a white man, and stepped aside to let the other pass. Nat's head movement caused the hated bell to sound just as he noticed the other person's feet deliberately move to block his path. The lamplight fell squarely on highly polished shoes—his father's.

"So," Elmo Travis said softly, "do you have a job at night going around ringing that bell for all your kind?"

Nat ignored the sarcasm and kept his eyes down and his answer short. "No, Massa." He didn't want to think why his father might be here in the quarters.

"My *son* and I," Travis continued, emphasizing the second word, "had originally planned to take you out of here Sunday after breakfast. But your young master wants you gone before then, as I'm sure you know. We'll all leave tomorrow."

Nat's head snapped up in spite of his training. "What?" The word popped out in his surprise.

Nat saw the hand as a flash out of the darkness, but the palm exploded against his cheek before he could even think to duck.

"You know better than to look at me, boy!"

Nat dropped his gaze, his eyes tearing up with the pain of the unexpected blow. "Sorry, Massa!" he whispered, trying to control a furious impulse to strike back.

"Don't ever forget it!" Elmo said sharply. "Now, get out of my way!"

"Yes, Massa," Nat replied, quickly stepping aside.

But his father didn't move. "One thing more," he said coldly, "when I buy an uppity one of your kind, my son and I like to make an example to show the other slaves what happens to the likes of you. So when you go out from here tomorrow, you'll be chained around the neck, the waist, and your wrists. You'll walk behind our buggy like a dog so that everyone on this plantation will never do anything as foolish as you did in running away!"

Elmo strode off into the night, leaving Nat raging inside. His father had made it clear that he was a slave, nothing more. Certainly not a son.

But they'll never take me out of here like that! he told himself. *I'll run tonight, even with this bell telling where I am!* He started to turn back to his shared cabin before he remembered Tolliver's supper invitation. *Run now?* Nat silently asked himself. *Or risk a couple of hours with Tolliver to see if I can learn something that may make William change his mind about selling me?*

Taking a slow, deep breath, Nat made his decision.

A PROMISE AND A PROBLEM

During the meager supper with Tolliver and his older friend Doris, Nat had a nagging feeling that he should have run away instead. He was sure that he had not been invited for a social matter, but for another.

That feeling grew through the evening, though Tolliver didn't press when Nat replied with only a shrug when asked about his reasons for running away before. Nat believed Tolliver already knew those reasons.

Doris was nearly deaf, so she rarely spoke as she prepared a typical meal of ground corn mixed with water. It was cooked with fatback over a "spider," a kind of frying pan on legs standing in the fireplace flames. With the meal almost over, Doris mixed meal and water into a thick dough prior to shaping them into hoecakes.

At a knock on the door, Nat looked up expectantly. He hoped Delia had come by as Tolliver had earlier hinted she might. Tolliver left Nat at the table, opened the door slightly, and slipped outside. Nat couldn't see who was there. He heard another male voice but no words.

Nat wondered who was outside with Tolliver. He tried to encourage himself with the hope that when his host returned, he might at least hint something about the planned slave revolt. Nat reasoned that perhaps he could trade that information to William in exchange for not selling him. If Tolliver didn't say anything, Nat would have lost valuable time in trying to run away before Travis carried out his threat about leading him away tomorrow.

When Tolliver returned to the crude table, his tone was nonchalant. He asked, "Mo' hog an' hominy?"

"No," Nat said, patting his stomach. "Dey's a-plenty in me now."

"Den how 'bout dem hoecakes?" Tolliver motioned toward Doris, who was cooking the delicacies on the flat side of a hoe stuck in the fireplace coals.

"Sho' do look good," Nat said.

After the hoecakes were eaten and Doris retired to the corner to smoke her pipe, Tolliver produced his own pipe and extended a tobacco pouch across the table. When Nat shook his head, Tolliver filled the pipe. But before lighting it, he used it to point to Nat's bell and collar, then in the direction of the big house.

"Dey do dat, so how much y'all hate dem?"

Nat hesitated. Not since his first master died and he had been sold away from his family had Nat found any reason to like white people except Emily and Gideon. He was ambivalent about Julie and deeply resented William's treatment. Most of all, Nat hated being in bondage, and that was because of white people. He finally shrugged without answering Tolliver's question.

Tolliver seemed satisfied and lowered his voice. "Y'all lak be rid dat bell an' be free?"

"Ain't no way," Nat said evasively.

"Oh, but dey is! Dey is. In de mornin,' befoh de horn blow, go outside."

"Why?"

Tolliver smiled through his curly beard. "Y'all see den, Nat. Jis' y'all wait!"

Nat didn't want to leave without learning something more, but he finally realized it wasn't going to happen. When he left, he stepped into the darkness where many questions buzzed around in his head. He decided he needed to talk to someone wiser than he, so he headed for the carriage house.

★ ★ ★ ★ ★

Gideon shoved the book Mrs. Yates had loaned him closer to the weak light from the coal-oil lamp. He read the first line again. *Call me Ishmael.*

Gideon was intrigued with the strange power those three words had in drawing him into Herman Melville's *Moby Dick*. Yet Gideon's mind kept slipping back to John Fletcher and Dilly. They had ridden the buckboard into the village to tell the sheriff what Dilly had learned about the tobacco pouch found after Gideon was chased in the swamp.

His mother looked up from where she was seated in her old hickory rocker to sew. "It's getting late. You had better get some sleep."

"I'm too excited to sleep. I'll wait until they get back." He left the open novel on the table, stood up, and faced his mother. "What do you think the sheriff will do now that Dilly's told him about the old slave woman who made that tobacco pouch?"

"I'd guess that he will go to Briarstone and find out if she's still alive, been sold, or what. Then he'll talk to her and find out who she was making it for."

"But that will take too long, Mama! It'll soon be Sunday, and what if those men hear about the tobacco pouch and decide to attack before then?"

"I'm sure Sheriff Geary will be very careful. But we've done all we can, except continue to wait and pray."

"I'd rather pray and do something at the same time," Gideon sighed.

"Then talk to me. Tell me what you've done to get ready to go to Richmond—*if* you really get the chance."

"Well, I've . . . Listen!" He stopped and cocked his head as the dogs suddenly bawled from under the back porch. "I think they're back!" He rushed for the door, eager to know the latest news.

★ ★ ★ ★ ★

Emily stood before Julie's bedchamber window and peered thoughtfully out into the night. Lamps still showed in the kitchen window and the harness shed. Darkness covered everything else.

"I should never have made that silly wager with your brother," she said without looking around. "Not that I'm afraid of losing, but it was just wrong to do."

"It's done, so stop punishing yourself," Julie replied from

where she was selecting clothes for tomorrow from the armoire. "Maybe that'll help you to understand why I keep most of my opinions to myself."

"But I can't do that!" Emily whirled around, her long blond hair cascading in a golden swirl around her face. "I have strong opinions, and I believe I'm right, so I've got to say what I think."

"Then you have to pay the price when your mouth gets you in trouble."

Emily hated to admit that, but she realized Julie was right. "I suppose," she confessed.

Julie closed the armoire door and turned with a clean dress over her arm. "It's like the biblical law of sowing and reaping."

Emily frowned. "I guess it is. I can't unsow what I did, but maybe I can do something about the reaping."

"What could you possibly do to prove that Nat isn't involved in this uprising business?"

"Maybe if I could talk to Nat . . ."

"Don't be ridiculous, Emily!" Julie exclaimed. "Proper white girls don't talk with field hands."

Before Emily could reply, she saw someone step from the darkness into the light from the carriage house. "I think that's Nat!" She watched him stop and peer in the window. "Yes, I'm sure it is."

Julie came over to stand beside Emily. "I don't see what he has in common with that old coachman."

"It doesn't matter," Emily declared, turning around and grabbing her cousin's hands. "This is my chance to talk to Nat. Come with me."

Julie drew back. "Oh no. William will have a fit if we did that. I won't go, and neither should you."

"Maybe not, but I'm going anyway!" She ignored her cousin's protests, grabbed her cloak, and dashed out of the room.

★ ★ ★ ★ ★

Nat stood outside the carriage room window, his right hand over the telltale bell to keep it silent. He wanted to be sure Uncle George was alone before making his presence known. It took several seconds before Nat glimpsed the old coachman emerging from behind the ornate town coach with a polishing cloth in hand. He began using it on gold mountings above the fancy Briarstone crest.

Satisfied that George was alone, Nat started to move on toward the door when a voice from behind stopped him.

"Nat, don't turn around!" Delia's voice was low as she added, "Somebody might be watching, so pretend you've got something wrong with your shoe."

He bent over and reached for his right foot, glad to hear Delia's voice, but he was aware that fear caused her to stay in the shadows.

She said in a hoarse whisper, "Someone told me that they overheard the trader threaten what he was going to do to you tomorrow. I went to the cabin where you had supper to tell you how sorry I was, but there was a man already there, knocking on the door. The one inside came out and they talked. I heard them say that somebody else wants you to join them in doing something. I didn't hear what it—Oh! Someone's coming! I'll try to tell you more later!"

Puzzled and greatly concerned, Nat stood up and scraped his shoe as if to make sure that whatever had been bothering him was gone.

"Oh!" a feminine voice cried. "You startled me!"

He spun around as Emily approached from the big house. "Please step out of the light," she whispered. "We must talk."

Nat gladly moved away from the window, but he was sorry to see her. He would suffer great punishment if he was caught alone with a white girl at night. "Please, Miss Emily," he said hoarsely, glancing around fearfully, "go back now!"

She stopped a few feet away, on the other side of the window. Her words came in a low rush. "I can't, not until I tell you something. William is convinced that you're part of a plot to kill and burn all of us!"

The unjust accusation instantly filled Nat with anger, but he controlled his emotions and spoke quietly. "You know that's not true, Miss Emily!"

"Of course I know! I told William that I'm positive you're not! He told me that he had originally ordered you to discover who *is* behind it, then tell him. When you didn't, he decided that you're the only one intelligent enough and with good reason to plan something like that."

"Please, Miss Emily," Nat whispered, "leave now!"

"One more thing," she replied. "If you won't do it for William, please do it for Julie, Gideon, and me. Then William will know you weren't involved."

Nat moaned inwardly, but Emily and Gideon had helped him and never asked anything in return. "All right," he whispered. "I'll do what I can."

"Thank you, Nat."

She silently left, leaving Nat with the realization that he might save the lives of Emily, Gideon, and Julie. *Now I can't run.* he realized. *But what about my own life?*

★ ★ ★ ★ ★

Gideon and his mother learned most of what the sheriff had said before they led Fletcher and Dilly into the kitchen. "He won't question anyone till early next week?" Gideon wailed. "What if those men attack this Sunday?"

"Well, as you know, Gideon," Fletcher answered, "the sheriff found the old woman who made the tobacco pouch after you passed on to him what Dilly told you. She remembered making it, and mentioned a Briarstone slave called Tolliver. Geary then had to come back to ask Dilly more questions, so now he's figured out what's going on."

Dilly declared, "I won't tell anyone."

"I know," Fletcher replied. "The sheriff also said that if any white man even talked to Tolliver, others involved would hear about it and know they'd been discovered."

"I see," Mrs. Tugwell said. "They might panic and attack right away."

"Exactly," Fletcher replied. "But if they don't suspect that the sheriff has any idea of who's involved, we might quietly round up all the conspirators."

Gideon asked, "Does he think there are more involved than the three who chased me?"

"There's no way of knowing until at least one of them talks," Fletcher explained, "and that's what the sheriff's plan is designed to do. But that person mustn't know his words are going to get back to Sheriff Geary."

"How's he going to do that?" Gideon wanted to know.

"He didn't say," Fletcher replied. "The fewer people who know about it, the fewer chances there are that word might leak out to the conspirators. There's a certain amount of risk, but the sheriff says all those conspirators must first be identified, then seized as close together as possible. We can't risk having anyone escape to try another uprising."

Gideon's mother worried, "What if Sheriff Geary is wrong and his plan doesn't work?"

"He said that in every slave uprising except Nat Turner's, someone inside the conspiracy betrayed the plan to the big house. William has already contacted Nat about finding out who's involved. That, with the sheriff's own investigation, will take a few days. Meantime, we've got no choice but to stay alert and hope this works."

Gideon closed his eyes to hide the sudden agony that he was afraid would show there. More delays, and he was running out of time to get everything done so he could leave for Richmond by September twenty-eighth.

"Well," his mother said, "let's hope there are no other complications."

Seeing Fletcher and Dilly exchange glances, Gideon asked sharply, "What is it?"

Fletcher started to shake his head, but Mrs. Tugwell reached out and gently touched the wrist where his left hand was missing. "Tell us," she urged.

The hired man took a deep breath and looked at Dilly, who gave a barely perceptible nod.

"All right." Fletcher turned to Gideon and his mother. "Dilly and I ran into some patrollers down the road. They said . . ."

"What?" Gideon prompted in dismay. "What?"

★ ★

"I don't want to alarm either of you," Fletcher answered softly, "but they had chased a Union cavalry patrol, which got away."

"Mercy!" Mrs. Tugwell cried. "Both Mrs. Yates and the sheriff warned us that patrols were close by, but Yankees! Oh, I pray they don't come here!"

★ ★ ★ ★ ★

George was seated inside the town coach dusting the seats when Nat stood outside the open carriage door and related his problems. His voice rose in anger as he finished. "Why? Why did my own father boast about how he was going to lead me away in chains like an animal?"

"Shh!" George cautioned, glancing around the carriage room where they were alone. "I can only guess."

Nat looked up into the old coachman's calm brown eyes and urged, "Then guess before I lose my mind."

"All right. Climb up in here and sit beside me."

As Nat stepped up into the coach, he realized that if he could get a ride away from Briarstone in this vehicle, there would be no scent for the hounds to follow. When the carriage passed a creek, Nat could jump out, wade awhile to further delay the dogs, and make his way to the swamp. From there, he knew where to contact the local "conductor" of the secret Underground Railroad.

No! Nat told himself. *Even if I got completely away, George would be punished. I can't do that to him.*

Nat looked expectantly at the old reinsman. "Go ahead," he said with forced calm. "I'm ready to listen."

THE RINGLEADER

George settled back against the carriage seat and regarded the younger slave with somber brown eyes. "I can only guess why Master Travis purposely hurt you by saying that tomorrow he was going to lead you away in chains like a dog."

"Tell me," Nat urged.

"Well, Master Travis's anger may be because he feels guilty about what he did to your mother when she was a girl. But he suppresses his conscience by lashing out at you, not willing to admit—even to himself—that you are his son."

Nat squirmed, recalling his mother telling him how she had come to bear him by a white man.

George continued, "It's also possible that Master Travis is afraid that Clement also saw the resemblance between you two boys. In that case, Master Travis might have threatened you to mislead Clement so he wouldn't say anything to his mother. You can imagine how a well-to-do Southern white woman would react to news like that."

Nat's anger surged. "So my father is so ashamed of having a son by a slave woman that he denies it to everyone, even himself?"

"I think that's likely," George admitted.

Nat slid off the seat and stepped to the carriage room floor. "Well, whatever his reason, I'd like to make him and his white son suffer the way I have! I never thought I'd say it, but I want revenge—not just on them, but for the injustice of slavery!"

"Easy, Nat!" George said, stiffly getting out of the carriage to face him. "Don't lose your common sense. You need to forgive, not seek revenge."

"I can't forgive this!" Nat flared. "That's one thing I can decide. A while ago, I couldn't even make up my mind whether to run away tonight or stay and let them humiliate me tomorrow. I was on my way to ask you to help me decide when Miss Emily stopped me outside your window. In just a few seconds, I promised that I'd try to find out what she wants. But right now I just want to avenge myself on my father and half brother, then escape."

"Revenge is never good, Nat. It's best to forgive, because sooner or later we all need to be forgiven."

Nat started to explode in disagreement but paused. "Have you forgiven those who condemned you to a lifetime of slavery? Is that why you stay calm and submissive?"

George nodded. "That, but I also have a glory."

Nat blinked. "A what?"

"A glory. On this plantation, I'm a slave. But in my heart, I am free."

"That doesn't make any sense to me!" Nat complained.

"I could explain it, but it would be better if you understood it for yourself. You said Delia had invited you to go with her Sunday night. Why don't you do that?"

Nat mused, "Maybe I will—if I'm still here."

★ ★ ★ ★ ★

Dawn was still a long way off when Nat clamped a hand over the bell on his collar and eased through the cabin of sleeping men. He had experienced a restless night of little sleep and thinking in circles. He had made no decision except to go outside before the horn blew. He had to learn what Tolliver meant at supper when he had mentioned getting rid of the bell and being free. The crisp autumn air felt good on Nat's face as he stood uncertainly in the predawn darkness, his hand still clenched over the bell. He smelled woodsmoke from fireplaces and saw a few candles lit in some slave cabin windows, but it was too dark to see anything else.

He heard a sound behind him and started to turn, but Tolliver's voice warned, "Don' look back. Go straight on, slow-like, an' listen. Don' talk."

With his hand still silencing the bell, Nat moved beyond all the slave cabins. He heard footsteps behind him until his nose told him he was near the pigpen. Fear of the unknown began to trouble Nat. He wished he had not come out here, but he fought misgivings in the hope that he was about to learn something of the planned uprising.

Nat was close enough to hear hogs grunting when Tolliver spoke again.

"Dat's good. Stop an' jis' listen."

Wordlessly, Nat obeyed.

Another voice came from near the smelly pigpen. "Y'all want be rid dat bell an' be free, slave boy?"

Nat recognized Harry's voice and visualized the big ugly *R* scar that had been burned into his left cheek. This had led to infection that malformed what had obviously once been his good looks.

"Yassuh," Nat replied.

"Y'all lak white fo'ks pay fo' what dey done to y'all?"

Nat's heart skipped a beat. "Yassuh."

"Den listen good." Harry's voice was so low it was difficult to hear him clearly. He began revealing an uprising plan that made Nat's heart leap into a gallop.

When Harry finished, Nat's mouth was so dry from fear that he felt as if his tongue would clack as he spoke. "When dis gwine be?"

Harry replied, "Only one man know dat, an' he won't even tell us. He say dat's how all dem uprisin' went bad, 'cause de massas foun' out. Nobody know but de main man. So is you wid us or no?"

Nat tried to speak casually. "De trader, he gwine take me dis day to sell me down de ribber. So—"

"He ain't gwine noplace fo' days," Tolliver broke in, sounding pleased. "We done fixed—"

"Shut yo' mou'f!" Harry interrupted harshly.

Tolliver muttered to himself but said no more.

Harry spoke again. "Nat, 'member dis: If'n y'all gwine tell anybody a'tall, y'all daid!"

★ ★

★ ★ ★ ★ ★

Emily had dressed and was trying to read her Bible before going down to breakfast, but she couldn't concentrate. She kept thinking of her foolish wager with William and what a thoughtless thing she had asked of Nat last night. She silently scolded herself.

I thought it was unfair of William to demand that Nat find out who's behind the uprising. Then I pleaded with Nat: If he wouldn't do it for William, do it for Julie, Gideon, and me. And to prove to William that Nat wouldn't betray us. I didn't think that his own life might be in danger, but it could be if those plotters find out what he promised me he would do.

Emily tensed at the sound of horses' hooves coming up the lane. She flew to the window of her bedchamber, recalling when foraging Union cavalry had pounded on the front door with musket butts and demanded food.

She took one glance and exclaimed aloud, "They're Confederates!" Her eyes skimmed the horsemen to see if her uncle Silas was leading this troop. He wasn't. These were all young men in their teens or early twenties. They looked older and very weary in their frayed uniforms. The ribs showed on some horses, and all plodded tiredly.

She turned at a sudden knocking at her door. "Emily! It's Julie! Our cavalry has come! They may have news!"

Emily didn't share her cousin's enthusiasm for the new arrivals, but she grabbed her cape and bonnet before opening the door.

"Hurry!" Julie urged, turning to brush by her maid in the hallway. "Maybe they'll even know where Papa is!"

Emily followed, hearing footsteps on the third floor where the slave trader and his son were moving around. Knowing that today they planned to take Nat away made Emily sigh with regret. Her mind jumped to wondering why the troopers had come to Briarstone.

★ ★ ★ ★ ★

Sheriff Geary arrived, accompanied by the two Tugwell hounds, just as Gideon and Dilly finished the barn chores and headed toward the house for breakfast. After all three exchanged greetings, Gideon asked, "Any news on the uprising?"

"Not yet, but I'm hoping."

Disappointed, Gideon commented, "You been out riding all night?"

"Most of it." The sheriff glanced at Dilly. "You never say much, do you?"

"No, suh," Dilly replied. "I jis' listen mostly."

"He's a hard worker," Gideon declared, then rushed on to ask, "Why were you out all night, Sheriff?"

"Checking with the patrollers. They've found signs of Union cavalry on some of the side roads."

"How about our troops?" Gideon asked.

"I just saw some riding this way. Most likely foragers. If so, they'll probably stop at Briarstone. Your family is so far back off the road they may not bother you. But you'd better alert John to be ready. Where is he?"

"He's in the far pasture but will be here shortly."

The door opened, and Mrs. Tugwell stepped out, drying her hands on an apron. "Join us for breakfast, Sheriff?"

He briefly lifted his slouch hat, revealing his balding pate. "No, thanks. I've got to get home."

She approached, asking, "Anything on the uprising?"

"No, but I just told the boys that there are signs of both Union and Confederate cavalry in this area."

Mrs. Tugwell's hand flew to her throat. "Do you think there'll be a battle around here?"

"No. These are small detachments, probably foraging for food for themselves and fodder for their horses. The fighting has been in Maryland."

"What happened there?" Gideon asked. "The last we heard was when Edwin Toombs told us that General Lee had invaded Maryland and there had been a big battle near a place called Antietam."

"It's a creek," the sheriff explained. "Yankees call it Sharpsburg because it was near that town. The wires report terrible losses on both sides. Nobody yet knows who won, but General Lee is pulling out of Maryland."

"Retreating?" Gideon asked in alarm.

The sheriff smiled. "We don't think of Lee as retreating. He's probably just pulling back to regroup before attacking again. You know he always attacks."

"Sure does!" Gideon exclaimed. "That's why he and Stonewall Jackson have beaten every Yankee general they've faced."

The sheriff nodded. "Well, take care of yourselves." He started to turn his mount around, then stopped. "Oh, Gideon, Mrs. Yates said if I saw you I should say that she heard back from her Richmond friend. She has no sleeping room for a boy, but she'll help you find a place and also board you in exchange for doing some yard work around her place."

Gideon's face lit up. "That's mighty fine! Now I know I won't starve while I'm there."

His mother cautioned, "You know there's not much time left before you have to leave, and you can't do that with this uprising still hanging over our heads."

"Ah, Mama! I want to go so much that I know this whole uprising is going to be stopped. Right, Sheriff?"

"I'm doing my best, Gideon." He lifted his hand in farewell and rode off.

Gideon looked at his mother and saw the worry in her tired face. "It'll be all right, Mama," he said, slipping his arms around her neck. "Another problem has just been solved, and the others will be, too. You'll see."

She nodded, but Gideon sensed she wasn't so sure.

★ ★ ★ ★ ★

Neither Tolliver nor Harry mentioned their predawn meeting with Nat as they harnessed the mules and entered the field to continue loading harvested tobacco leaves. Nat assumed they were unwilling to risk anyone possibly overhearing anything about the uprising. Or perhaps their silence was to reinforce the threat on Nat's life.

He had stopped thinking in circles and had come to a conclusion. *Julius has to be the leader in this planned uprising. He's the only logical one who could control Harry and Tolliver and send them to ask if I'd join the Rebellion. That's probably why Julius suddenly started being nice to me. But I can't tell Emily or William that without proof. There's no time to get that because my father plans to take me away today. Unless Tolliver is right, and we can't leave for some reason I can't figure.*

Looking around for Julius, Nat saw him walking back from where William and the white overseer sat on their mounts and talked at the end of the tobacco rows. Julius briefly looked at Nat, then away. He was sure that Julius had been watching him since daylight. That didn't surprise him after Tolliver and Harry's predawn talk.

Julius has to be the leader, Nat told himself with growing conviction. *But are there others involved in the plot besides him, Harry, and Tolliver?*

Nat could only wait and watch for the answer, but he knew that if he did anything to make them suspicious, he would end up dead. He forced that thought aside as other questions spun in his head.

When he, Harry, and Tolliver returned to the drying barn with a load of tobacco leaves, they left him alone. They walked over to get a drink from the little slave girl who had started back toward the fields with a wooden bucket of water for field hands. The two men stood with their backs to Nat. He looked toward the big house just as a detachment of Confederate cavalrymen slowly rode up the long lane.

A quick look back to the fields disclosed William and his white overseer still talking, unaware of the new arrivals. Glancing back toward the big house, Nat saw Emily and Julie emerge from inside and step out onto the lawn to await the oncoming soldiers.

"Nat."

He spun around. "Delia!" She had come up behind him so quietly he hadn't heard her approach. She stood beside the sledge, using the high piles of broad leaves to shield her from Harry and Tolliver.

She whispered, "You're in terrible danger!"

★ ★ ★ ★ ★

Entering the house behind his mother, Gideon tried to convince her to see the Richmond trip from his viewpoint. "I've still got nine days to get the money before I have to leave. I figure on three days' travel, so I've got to be on my way by Sunday the twenty-eighth."

"That's assuming the uprising is stopped," she said, "and that the roads aren't blocked by artillery or troops. It'll be much worse if it rains. What if those heavy wheels, horses' hooves, and human footprints turn the roads into axle-deep mud again?"

Gideon hung his hat and jacket on the peg behind the door. "You really don't want me to go, do you?"

"You're not quite fourteen, and I'm torn between wanting you to have a chance at making your dreams come true and my mother's heart, which doesn't want anything bad to happen to you."

"Nothing's going to happen—" He broke off as heavy footsteps sounded on the back porch and John Fletcher entered, grinning.

"While I was in the far corner of the pasture by the swamp, I heard a hog squealing. You've caught him, but we'd better hitch Hercules to the sledge and haul that trap back here before he tears it up."

"I'm on my way!" Gideon cried, dashing out the door and calling for Dilly to come help him.

A BRIEF REPRIEVE

Emily was startled at the transformation in the Confederate cavalrymen when they saw the girls walking to meet them. Dirty and in ragged uniforms, the young riders had been slumped wearily in their saddles. Instantly, as one man, they sat up straight in their frayed jackets and grinned at the girls.

Emily knew that they were enemies of the Union she supported. Yet they were also barely more than boys who would ride their skinny horses into battle to valiantly fight and die for their cause. She curtsied politely to the young officer riding ahead of the others. "Good morning. Do you bring news?"

He replied, "Lieutenant Daniel Comstock, Fifth Virginia Cavalry." He swept his hat off with a flourish and bowed slightly in the saddle. "My compliments to the master. Is he at home?"

Julie quickly dropped a curtsy and smiled demurely up at the young officer. "No, Lieutenant Comstock. My father is leading a cavalry unit of our gallant soldiers against the Yankees. My mother is indisposed, but my brother and I welcome you to Briarstone Plantation."

"Thank you, Miss. . . ?"

"Julie Lodge, *Miss* Julie Lodge. May I present my cousin, *Miss* Emily Lodge?"

Each trooper's smile widened to a grin of admiration.

Comstock fixed deep brown eyes on her. "You have an unusual accent, Miss Emily."

"She's my Yankee cousin from Illinois!" Julie declared quickly. "She lives with us. Please, step down. Have some refreshments while servants water your horses."

"Thank you, Miss Julie," the lieutenant replied. He dismounted and motioned for his men to do the same. They crowded around the girls, obviously starved for sight of two such pretty ones.

"Lodge?" Comstock mused, following the girls toward the front entrance to Briarstone. "By chance, are you any relation to Colonel Silas Lodge?"

"He's my father!" Julie cried. "Have you seen him?"

"Yes, more than a week ago. He was leading his men to join General Lee. As perhaps you heard, he invaded Maryland to fight the Yankees. The wires said there was a terrible battle day-before-yesterday at Antietam—" Comstock broke off, his face sobering. "Oh! Beggin' your pardon! I shouldn't have said—"

"Something happen to Papa?" Julie interrupted.

"I don't know, miss. We weren't there." Comstock added quickly, "But I'm sure he's all right."

Julie stepped up on the front steps between the white Corinthian columns, from one of which hung the red, white, and blue Confederate flag with its circle of seven white stars. She told the officer, "We heard there was a battle but had few details."

Julie turned to Emily. "Would you mind telling the servants to prepare refreshments while I catch up on news about Papa?" Without waiting for a reply, Julie swung around to again face the lieutenant. She urged, "Please tell me everything you know about seeing my father."

Emily hurried inside as the young riders clustered around Julie. Emily wondered what news the troopers brought about the battle at Antietam.

★ ★ ★ ★ ★

The annoying bell that rang incessantly at Nat's every move deepened his resentment at his lot in life. He managed to hide those feelings as he returned to the field with Harry and Tolliver on the empty sledge.

Nat asked, "How y'all know dey ain't gwine take me outa heah dis mornin'?"

Harry and Tolliver exchanged glances and grinned before Harry turned to Nat. " 'Cause in de night, dat ol' buggy dey come in done got all busted up!"

Nat sighed audibly. At least he had a few more days before he would be sold. But his relief was brief.

Harry asked in a low voice, "Y'all wid us or no?"

There had been no preamble, but Nat understood that Harry meant about joining the uprising. Nat didn't want any part of it, but he wasn't ready to say so, especially since Delia had warned that he was in danger. "I'se gwine over it in here." He tapped his forehead.

"You ain't got much mo' time," Tolliver warned.

Harry said, "Don' pay him no mind, Nat. You jis' lemme know soon's y'all kin."

Nat nodded, grateful that he still had some time. But the plotters probably would not wait that long for his decision. He was fearful of what would happen if he turned them down.

★ ★ ★ ★ ★

Gideon, Fletcher, and Dilly had finished getting the runaway hog out of the badly torn-up trap and into its pen when Sheriff Geary rode up on his horse. After he congratulated them on catching the animal, he explained why he had come by.

"Dilly, I found that old mammy you said made that tobacco sack you found in the swamp. She swore that she made it some years back for a Briarstone field hand named Harry. Do any of you know him?"

"Don't think so," Gideon replied. "Does that mean you think he's one of the three men who chased me?"

"It seems likely, so I'm following it up, but very quietly in hopes of not alerting any of the Briarstone slaves. I think that's possible because that woman is so old and weak, the only one who really sees her is another old slave woman who takes care of her. Both promised me that they wouldn't tell anyone I was asking questions."

"I hope something happens soon," Gideon declared. "Time's running out for me to get to Richmond on time."

The sheriff regarded Gideon with somber eyes. "You still think you're going to get to that interview?"

"I'm praying and working hard, believing that I am," Gideon replied.

Geary smiled and reached into his saddlebag. "Mrs. Yates told me that you'd say that. So she asked me to give you this." He handed an envelope down to Gideon. "It's from her friend Mrs. Stonum in Richmond. She's found a room for you, with board."

"Please thank Mrs. Yates for me!" Gideon exclaimed.

Fletcher grinned. "Well, Gideon, at least you know you'll have a roof over your head and food to eat if you do get there. But you still don't have pocket money or transportation for the trip."

"I'll get them," Gideon declared, sounding more sure than he really felt.

Geary asked the same question often posed to Gideon before. "If you do, and you get the job, what then?"

Shrugging, Gideon admitted, "I guess that's a bridge we can't cross until we get there."

Fletcher asked, "What's the latest war news?"

"Two days ago," Geary replied, "the bloodiest battle of the war was fought at Antietam in Maryland. This morning's wire reports almost twenty-eight thousand on both sides killed, wounded, or missing. We had the heaviest casualties because General Lee was badly outnumbered, yet he and his generals stopped five major Federal drives."

Fletcher asked, "Does that mean we won?"

"Nobody knows yet," Geary replied. "Some of our boys fought barefooted because they're short of everything."

Gideon's older half brother served with General Lee. He silently prayed that Isham was safe. Gideon excused himself and walked away to read Mrs. Stonum's letter, even though he already knew what it said. He told himself with fierce determination, *We've got to stop this uprising, so my family and friends will be safe and I can leave for Richmond by the twenty-eighth.*

★ ★ ★ ★ ★

At the drying barn, Harry produced his newly made tobacco pouch and told Nat that he and Tolliver were going to smoke behind the barn. That was strictly forbidden, but it wasn't Nat's concern, so he began unloading tobacco and carrying it to the slave women.

Nat was pleased to see that Delia was just inside the door, expertly tying three broad leaves with twine onto a notched stick. The leaves would later be cured with heat from logs supplied by a slave who sat up all night to keep the wood fire going.

After Harry and Tolliver were out of sight, Nat carried some leaves to Delia. He whispered, "What did you mean when you said that I'm in danger?"

She glanced around before whispering back, "They want you to help them, but they won't let you escape with them into the swamp."

Nat drew back. "How do you know?"

"I can't tell you, but trust me. They'll leave you behind with the others. . . ." She broke off as an older slave woman approached. Raising her voice, Delia switched to dialect. "Y'all gwine to de meetin' Sundee night?"

Nat nodded, watching in disappointment as the older woman settled beside Delia and began tying leaves. Nat desperately wanted to know more from Delia. However, there was no chance now. At least today he wouldn't be led away by his father and half brother.

Still, Nat faced a fearful dilemma. If he refused to go along with the uprising, the plotters would surely not let him live. But if Delia was right, his life would still be forfeit. Yet he knew that he couldn't have any part in harming Emily, Gideon, and the others.

Nat was tempted to think it would serve his father and Clement right if they were attacked, but he silently rebuked himself for even thinking that. He returned to the sledge, knowing he was soon going to have to choose, and either way he would lose. But he wasn't the only one.

★ ★ ★ ★ ★

Emily had mixed feelings that night after she and Julie sent their maids away so the girls could speak privately in Julie's bedchamber. They avoided talking about the Confederates' frightening report on Antietam.

Julie fingered the back of her dark hair against her neck. She wistfully said, "I can't get over how cute that lieutenant was! When he asked for a lock of my hair—"

" 'To wear next to my heart,' " Emily interrupted, deepening her voice to imitate Comstock's words.

"I wonder if he'll write as he said he would?"

Emily shrugged. "Well, you gave him your address."

"But you wouldn't give yours to anyone," Julie said disapprovingly. "And you were rude not to give them a lock of your hair when they asked."

Emily laughed. "If I gave a lock of my hair to every passing soldier, I'd be bald! Besides, you know I can't do anything against my conscience."

"You and your Yankee conscience! You saw how bad off those boys were. Some of their toes were sticking out of their boots. It's coming on winter, and not one of them had a warm coat. And their poor, half-starved horses. Well, at least William gave them better mounts and all the food they could carry. Oh, those poor, brave boys!"

"I hate this cruel war!" Emily exclaimed. "If they're right about what happened at Antietam . . ." She let her voice trail off.

"You thinking of your friend's brother, wondering if he was there and among the casualties, the same as I'm wondering about my father?"

Emily nodded. "Brice Barlow is very dear to me. Of course, I also feel the same about Uncle Silas. I know how you must worry about him, too, especially since the lieutenant said he joined Lee's forces before Antietam."

The girls momentarily fell silent, wondering about those mentioned, plus all their male friends they had known before the war.

Emily took a deep breath and slowly let it out. "It's hard right now, but I have faith in God that this war will someday end, and they'll all be back safe. I'll be home in Illinois again where I really want to be."

"I hope you're right, but it won't matter to us if this revolt isn't stopped in time."

Emily declared firmly, "It's going to be stopped!"

Their conversation switched to how furious William had been upon finding that Mr. Travis's buggy had been totally destroyed in the night.

Julie observed, "My brother believed that Nat had some others wreck the buggy. Nat couldn't do it without being heard because of that bell he wears. This all makes William even more convinced that Nat is the plot leader."

Emily defended him. "I'm sure he's innocent."

"Innocent or guilty, our unwelcome guests can't leave until they can buy a new buggy." Julie shook her head. "I wish they had accepted William's offer to let them take one of our other carriages. But Clement said there would be no way they could return it from Richmond." She paused before adding, "You should be happy that Nat will be around for at least another few days."

"I am," Emily admitted. "It gives me more time to prove William is wrong, and I can win that silly wager I made with him."

★ ★ ★ ★ ★

On Saturday, Gideon's and Emily's tensions were high, suspecting that tomorrow the plotters might strike. Nat believed that since neither Harry nor Tolliver had again approached him for his decision, the unknown leader did not plan to strike for a while. His father and half brother were still at Briarstone, even though they had borrowed one of William's light carriages and unsuccessfully searched for a new buggy. The war had halted their manufacture, so even used ones were hard to find.

Nat was greatly relieved when a fast-moving thunderstorm on Sunday morning seemed to almost ensure that the uprising would not take place. Rain might douse the fires the plotters had in mind for Briarstone and the Tugwells' home. Even though precipitation would wash out the scent so the dogs couldn't follow the fugitives after they struck and fled, muddy tracks might linger to be followed by the sheriff and hordes of angry neighbors who would surely rise up to avenge the massacre.

Nat was right. Nothing unusual happened that day. He was sure that there were great sighs of relief from within the big house and over at the Tugwells' small home.

Nat's anger at his father and half brother still remained high when darkness fell that evening. Nat slipped into the woods to meet Delia at the slave church services. It was the first time he had been able to speak to her since Thursday at the drying barns. He was eager to learn more of what she knew about the uprising and try to confirm that Julius was the leader.

Delia greeted him warmly when he sat down next to her on a split log. The singing promptly started, and she joined in before he could ask her anything. The dark woods rang with the deeply emotional and joyful voices accompanied by enthusiastic handclapping.

Nat quickly noticed that these services were quite unlike the somber Sunday morning rituals which most white owners required their slaves to attend. There the whites stiffly sat in upholstered pews down front. Slaves were either seated on hard benches in the far back or in a balcony.

Soon Delia was swaying from side to side, her eyes closed, her face radiant in the dancing torchlights. When the singing and shouting was over, she sat down and again smiled at Nat. He started to whisper his question to her, but she laid her forefinger across her mouth. "Shh! Brother Tynes is going to speak." She turned to face a small black man not over five feet tall, with curly gray hair and a smooth, dark face. He stepped upon a stump, his eyes reflecting fire from the pine torches.

"Hear what de Lord done say 'bout fergivin' dem dat do y'all wrong," he began.

Nat groaned. *I don't want to hear this!*

"But I say to y'all, love yo' en'mies, bless dem dat cuss ye, do good to dem dat hates y'all, an' pray fer dem dat use an per'cute y'all," Tynes quoted.

Nat looked at Delia and decided he couldn't leave her without trying to learn what she had meant earlier in warning him that he was in danger. *I'll stay because of that,* he told himself, *but I won't listen!*

16

AS TENSIONS RISE

After the slaves' secret church service, Nat walked back through the woods with Delia. He asked, "How do you know about those men's plans for me?"

Her face was invisible in the darkness, but Nat sensed her looking up at him to say, "You don't believe me, do you?"

"I'm just curious, that's all."

"First, tell me what you thought of Brother Tynes' sermon."

Nat stopped in surprise and reached out to take her hands to halt her. "If my life is in danger as you say, that's more important than what that preacher said."

"I've watched you closely, and I've seen the bitterness in your eyes about being sold to that slave trader."

"That doesn't answer my question," Nat argued. "But yes, I am bitter. Not just because I'm being sold like a dog. There's more to it than that, but I can't talk about it."

"I noticed that during the sermon you squirmed like you'd sat on an anthill. I believe you felt guilty because you think someone's done you wrong and you can't forgive them. Am I right?"

The sermon *had* disturbed him. He didn't want to forgive his father and half brother. He said, "I don't want to talk about it." He resumed walking without letting go of Delia's hand.

Moving with him, she asked, "You do believe in the Lord, don't you?"

"I never thought much about it."

"But now you are, and your conscience bothers you."

"I told you I don't want to talk about it!"

"Does it bother you that much?"

He stopped abruptly and released her hand. "All right! I am mad at the world because . . . well, because of something terrible that is being done to me by someone who shouldn't. So I've got a right to hate!"

Delia didn't answer for a moment, then spoke very softly. "Remember what Brother Tynes said about God our Father won't forgive us if we don't forgive our brother?"

"Brother? Father?" Nat's voice rose angrily. "Well, I won't forgive . . . uh . . . anybody . . . for what they've done to me! In fact, I want vengeance for the injustice they're doing! So don't ask me to think of forgiveness!"

He left Delia in high agitation and strode alone through the dark woods toward the slave quarters. But he turned aside and stopped at the carriage house, where the hated bell announced his arrival.

George opened the door, holding a broken piece of harness. "Your face looks a storm cloud. What's wrong?"

"Nothing I want to talk about. Tell me, what did you mean the other night when you told me you had a 'glory'?"

George motioned for the youth to enter, saying, "I'm not sure you're in the mood to understand."

"I'm hurting all over, Uncle George! All kinds of feelings are stirred up inside, and I don't like it. But I've never known you to be angry or upset over anything. If that's your 'glory,' I want to know how you got it and kept it through sixty years of being a slave."

"Sixty-three, near as I can figure," George replied. He hung the broken harness on a wall peg and motioned for Nat to enter the big town carriage. George stiffly climbed in to sit beside Nat before he continued.

"It's the way I look at things, Nat. When I was a boy, my mother—before they sold me away from her when I was about five or six—taught me that people tend to act the way they really believe. I believe that this place is not my real home. One day I'll be free of this earth's bonds; then I'll go to be with my heavenly Father. So faith gives me a glory inside. I try to show that outside by the way I live."

That was difficult for Nat to believe. But his own mother's teachings echoed in his mind. *"The mind is very powerful,"* she had declared. *"It's even stronger than the physical. Yet there is a connection, for what is deep in the well of the mind comes up in the bucket of behavior. What we believe, we prove to ourselves."*

Nat realized that his mother, although a slave, was very wise. George's mother must have been, too. George believed in the Lord and lived that belief.

After several seconds, George said, "Nat, you can have that same glory if you want."

Nat hadn't expected any of this. He shifted in the seat, placing his hands on the seat cushion near the backrest. His fingers touched something metallic, which he quickly recognized as keys.

George had no keys. No one rode in this town coach except William and his family. When Nat had worked in the big house, he had never seen William's mother with keys. Those Nat had found must belong William, who had probably lost them on the ride to church this morning. A thought flashed across Nat's mind: *Could one of these fit my bell collar?* Quietly he closed his fingers around the keys and eased them into his pocket. "Thanks for talking to me," he said. "I've got a lot to think about, so I'd better get over to the quarters."

George nodded as Nat stepped down from the carriage. "Come back anytime if you want to talk some more."

Nat thanked him and walked out into the night. His heart beat faster as he looked for a quiet place to try the keys. *If one of them opens this collar, and I get rid of this bell,* he told himself, *then I can run away—but that would mean breaking my promise to Miss Emily*.

Nat clamped his hand around the bell to silence it, then slipped round to the barn. After listening and hearing no human sounds, he climbed into the haymow. Barely able to breathe, he tried the first key in the lock on his bell collar.

★ ★ ★ ★ ★

Monday morning Gideon awakened at dawn, grateful that there had been no uprising the day before. Now it seemed likely that it would not happen until the following Sunday. That was the last day he could leave and be in Richmond in time for the interview. But he couldn't go unless he overcame three remaining obstacles: Stop the revolt, obtain transportation, and get some spending money.

He dressed and stepped out onto the back porch just as the rooster started crowing. From the shadows under the porch, he heard Fletcher's quiet voice. Gideon jumped like a startled deer. "How long you been there?"

"Long enough." Fletcher struck a match and lit the lantern. The light reflected off of a pistol in his belt and a shotgun leaning against the post near at hand. He explained, "I brought them when I left my quarters in the barn, just in case I was wrong and the uprising is today. You ready to start the chores?"

"Maybe I should first ride over and make sure that Emily and the others are all right."

"Look over toward Briarstone. Lamps have been lit in the lower floor where the servants are up, but there's no light on the second and third bedchamber floors. That means everything's all right there."

"You're right," Gideon agreed, reaching for the milk bucket, which was turned upside down on a shelf against the outside kitchen wall. He fell into step with the hired man, saying, "I'm glad yesterday's rain stopped. I know we're going to have lots more, but I hope it holds off until I get to Richmond."

They passed the pigpen as Fletcher said, "You still need some spending money, plus transportation."

"I know! I know!" Gideon didn't mean to sound desperate, but what he felt inside showed in his tone.

"If I could," Fletcher continued, "I'd give you the money. But I don't have it any more than your mother does. I'm sorry that I can't offer any transportation help, either. With no horses and only one mule—"

"I know," Gideon cut in. "Can't farm without Hercules. But I still have six days to get everything."

★ ★

The cow bawled as Fletcher swung open the heavy barn door. It was obvious to Gideon what Fletcher thought. Even if the slave revolt was stopped, there was no known way to overcome those last two major obstacles.

The transportation issue was likely to become even more difficult. Seasonal rains would fall more often. Yesterday's rain had made the dirt road slippery on the wagon ride into church. But if rains got heavier, the roads between the Tugwell farm and the capital could soon turn to mud. It could even be hub deep if heavy wheeled cannon and countless foot soldiers passed. Three days might not be enough travel time if that happened.

Gideon groaned at the thought as he picked up the milk stool and sat down at the cow's right side. *There's got to be a way! But how?*

★ ★ ★ ★ ★

Emily had slept well, unlike Saturday night when she lay awake, fearful that the plotters might attack. She had heard nothing from Nat, which she assumed meant he had not learned anything.

She and Julie had gladly ridden through the rain to attend church with William and his mother. She had not been told about the possible uprising because her son forbade it, fearful that such news might worsen her delicate health.

Mr. Travis and Clement were just getting up when the family returned from services, where there were many silent prayers of gratitude. By then, however, William was fuming because he couldn't find his keys. Assuming that he had lost them at a neighboring plantation, he sent his body servant to have George harness the team and bring the town coach around.

★ ★ ★ ★ ★

Nat was surprised on Monday when neither Harry nor Tolliver said anything about joining them. Nat was just as glad because he felt exhilarated after yesterday. He still wore the bell, though unlocked, but he left it in place for appearances' sake.

Yesterday his conscience had been bothering him for fear that

George might get in trouble over William's lost keys. Nat had volunteered to help George wash the coach, which had been mud splattered from taking the master's family to the village church. Unknown to the old man, Nat had slipped the keys back into the crack between the seat cushion and the backrest where he had found them. He had just finished when Levi, William's body servant, arrived to tell George to bring the carriage around again.

Nat thought about that on Monday morning while he helped bring in tobacco from the fields. *Close!* Nat told himself. *If Levi had come a moment earlier, I couldn't have returned the keys. Now I can run—but what about my promise to help Emily find out about this uprising?*

★ ★ ★ ★ ★

As the days passed, Emily's apprehension grew. By Thursday morning, she had a difficult time remaining calm. Only two more days remained to stop the uprising, which almost certainly would happen on Sunday. She had not heard from Nat, and Gideon hadn't come by. She knew that only pressing farm work would keep him away because his tensions must be as high as hers. To add to her agitation, the slave trader and his son still had been unable to buy a rig. They claimed that buggies were now so scarce that prices were greatly inflated, and Travis refused to pay them.

It was nearing noon when Emily strolled alone down to the stables. Some of the Confederate cavalrymen who had ridden through days before had exchanged their skinny, broken-down mounts for some of Briarstone's blooded horses. While Emily absently stroked the velvet nose of one horse, Julie was tending to her ailing mother, and George and William rode the coach toward the village.

I don't see how this war can go on much longer, Emily thought. *It's not just the battles, but the Union naval blockade that's slowly strangling the South to death. I don't wish any harm to the people of the Confederacy, but I wish this were over so I could return to Illinois. . . .*

The unmistakable sound of horses' hooves and the squeak of saddle leather interrupted her musings. "Oh no! Not again!" she muttered, hurrying to look out of a barn window toward the big house.

She took one glance and sucked in her breath. It was not Confederate cavalry this time, but a detachment of Federals. They looked so splendid in their crisp blue jackets and red stripes down their trouser legs that Emily felt a surge of pride. Everything about them was in sharp contrast to the ragtag Confederate cavalrymen.

The Union leader stood in his stirrups, waved a newspaper, and called loudly to the few slaves working outside the big house. "Listen to me! On Monday of this week, President Lincoln issued an official Emancipation Proclamation setting all slaves free! It's written right here in this newspaper!"

Aunt Anna! Emily thought. *If she hears this, it might frighten her to death, and Julie is too timid to rebuke that soldier!* Emily yanked her hoopskirt up above her shoe tops and ran toward the officer, who looked to be in his midtwenties.

He didn't see her and continued shouting. "It says that every slave held in states now in rebellion against the Union is free as of the first day of January 1863. That's just a little more than three months away. But if you'll leave with us, you'll find food and shelter waiting for you in our lines. Come with us so my men and I can protect—"

"Sir!" Emily interrupted, making him turn to face her. He wore the three bars of a captain. "Please keep your voice down! My aunt is very ill. You'll upset her with all your shouting."

The officer's blond eyebrows arched wide over blue eyes. "Well, what do we have here? A sesesh gal!"

"I'm no secessionist!" Emily replied firmly, drawing near. "I'm from Illinois, and I support President Lincoln and the Union cause. I'm an orphan living with relatives in this house. Please be considerate of my ailing aunt, and don't trouble these poor people." She motioned toward the curious slaves. She was conscious that all of the cavalrymen were smiling at the sight of her and perhaps surprised at her spirit. The captain studied her with cool eyes.

"Miss, I admit you don't speak like Rebels I've heard, but it doesn't matter. My men are foraging for supplies. We require keys to the peripheries, especially the smokehouse. We must also enter this house to search for weapons."

"You'll do no such thing!" Emily scolded, her eyes bright with sudden anger. "My cousin William, who's master of this plantation, is away. But if you act like gentlemen and stop stirring up these poor people, you'll be given what we can spare in Christian charity."

For a moment, the officer tried to stare her down. Failing that, he shrugged. "Here. Take this paper. It tells all about the Emancipation Proclamation. I must assume that you haven't heard, because it was officially announced after our victory at Sharpsburg. My men will not enter your house, but we do insist on taking the supplies we need."

"Not without me along!" Emily declared firmly. "If you are true Union gentlemen, you'll do me the favor of doing as I wish."

A grin slowly spread across the captain's face. "You win, miss, because we are gentlemen."

Emily took a very long, deep breath, then smiled up at all the young cavalrymen. They returned her smile. She exhaled, saying, "Then, gentlemen, please follow me."

★ ★ ★ ★ ★

Julie, Mr. Travis, and Clement rushed out of the house just as the Federals rode down the long lane with hams, bacon, and live hens slung across their saddles. The yard slaves still stood in sullen silence as the raiders entered the public road and loped away to the west.

Emily finished telling Julie, Mr. Travis, and Clement what had happened when George and William returned from the east. He stepped out of the carriage, saying, "I found my keys—"

"Yankees were here!" Julie broke in. She rushed on breathlessly, repeating what Emily had told her. "He left this Yankee newspaper about the battle at Antietam," Julie concluded, "and the Emancipation Proclamation."

Emily watched the anger darken William's face as he skimmed the publication. "That's a lie!" he exclaimed to his relatives and the two visitors. "The Yankees didn't win at Antietam, or Sharpsburg, as they call it. General Lee did. He didn't retreat, either, but just pulled his troops out of Maryland to fight somewhere else!"

Turning to the moody slaves, he called out, "Those Yankees also lied to you! Bluecoats kill black people! They don't care for you the way we in the South do. Even if you were all free, how would you support yourselves?

"You have no money, no land, no mules! You are far better off working for me. Here you have food to eat, roofs over your heads, and Sundays off. Forget what those lying Yankees said. Now, go enjoy the day and be grateful that you have a caring master to watch over you!"

Emily watched as the slaves slowly returned to their work, their faces less brooding. Julie continued filling William in on details she had heard about the Yankees. Mr. Travis and Clement joined in, but Emily walked away.

I wonder how news of the Emancipation Proclamation will affect the uprising? Why haven't I heard from Nat? Surely by now he must know something. If the plotters do as we think they will, there's only tomorrow and Saturday left before . . . She shuddered, unwilling to finish that thought.

★ ★

THE NIGHT BEFORE

On Saturday night, just hours before the expected slave uprising, Emily and Julie joined Sheriff Geary and William behind closed library doors. The officer shook his partially bald head in response to William's question.

"No, I'm sorry to say. Except for knowing that your man Harry once owned that tobacco pouch and recently has a new one, we don't know much more than we did at the beginning. Oh yes, that old slave woman did tell me that she remembered when your father punished both Harry and Tolliver, so that could be their motive—if they are involved in the conspiracy."

William protested, "They should not hold anything against me for what my father did. Just the same, to be safe, I'll have Toombs, my overseer, keep an eye on Harry. He and Tolliver work together with Nat, which helps convince me that Nat's the leader."

Emily declared, "Sheriff, I don't think Nat is involved in any way."

William scowled at her, then looked back to the sheriff. "But if Emily is right and Nat isn't involved, which I sincerely doubt, I'm hesitant to move against Harry and Tolliver without proof, especially without knowing if there are others involved besides Massie."

William paused and glanced back at Emily. "You made me see that Massie's repeated eavesdropping meant she logically had to remain under suspicion. My own investigation convinced me that the other house servants are loyal, so Massie has to be the spy inside this house."

Emily nodded slightly, surprised that William had admitted listening to her about anything.

"Everyone must be caught," he continued, "so I can't even risk moving tonight because word might get out to the plotters, and they could postpone the attack."

"I agree," Geary said, "but whether you're right or wrong about Nat, whoever the leader is has apparently not told anyone much."

William frowned. "What really surprises me is that none of the servants have told me a thing. They love to receive little trinkets in exchange for information about the others, but that hasn't worked this time. Of course, it's also possible that followers are afraid to talk."

Emily commented, "Whoever the leader really is, he must have recruited others. It would take more than one person to successfully attack six of us." She glanced around at each of them before adding, "That's counting Aunt Anna, Mr. Travis, and Clement. So even if whoever it is struck some of us, there's always the chance that there'd be a scream or other commotion."

"I agree," Geary replied. "But there's no way of knowing how many of them there are."

"I still think that Nat is the only one with enough motive and intelligence to plan this," William said. "I'm glad Mr. Travis and Clement finally bought a used buggy today so they can take Nat away tomorrow. To be safe, I'll have him chained until they're ready to leave."

"Chain him?" Emily exclaimed in dismay.

"Yes, chain him!" William's voice rose angrily. "He's my property, and I can do anything I want with him! Now, you stay out of this. In fact, you and Julie had better leave. The sheriff and I will handle this alone."

Stunned, Emily walked out, recalling the summer she had seen Nat tied to a whipping post while William lashed his bare back. Now it was autumn. Exposure alone would not kill Nat if he was chained all night, but he might catch cold or even die of pneumonia.

Emily's mind raced. *Would it be wrong if I warned Nat? If I did, what could he do except run away where the slave catcher and his dogs might get him?*

★ ★ ★ ★ ★

At the sound of the banjo player tuning up in Briarstone's barn, Nat took a deep breath and decided.

Tonight. It's a full moon—a good night for running away. If I get into the swamp before the hounds get me, I can make it to the Underground Railroad station. If I don't hear the hounds before I leave the swamp, maybe I can find my little brother. We could escape together.

There were two urgent reasons for his decision. This afternoon, he had seen Travis and Clement return with a used buggy. Tomorrow they would surely start him on the way to the Deep South. Harry and Tolliver were waiting for Nat's answer about joining them. If he said he had decided against it, they wouldn't let him live.

So I've got no choice, Nat assured himself as he entered the building for the slaves' traditional Saturday night dance. *But I feel really terrible that I can't keep my promise to Miss Emily.*

He still liked the idea of trying to hang on to the back of the town coach and jump off into a creek so there would be no scent trail from Briarstone for the dogs to follow. But William might blame George for being an accomplice if it was ever known how Nat escaped. He could not risk that happening to George. Nat could only hope for a head start before he was missed and they came after him.

He concluded that the best time to run was during the dance. After he established that he was there, and when the revelry was at its highest, loudest pitch, he could slip out. After throwing away the bell, his absence might not be noticed until morning.

The music was lively and the crowd was joyful as the slaves tried to forget their hard life in the few hours of unsupervised relaxation. But Nat felt miserable. He glanced around at the blazing pine knots illuminating a ring where men and women field hands, dressed in their finest clothes, were starting to move in rhythm to the banjo's lively tempo.

Nat's eyes were drawn to Delia, whose back was turned to him. He gulped in surprise to see how pretty she was in her red dress. He leaned against the barn wall, his full attention on Delia, when someone stopped beside him.

"Dis de las' time, Nat. Is y'all wid us or no?"

Nat turned to look at Harry. He had spoken softly, yet there was a hardness to his tone. Although they daily worked together, neither Harry nor Tolliver had said anything to Nat after the predawn conversation by the pigpen a week ago.

"Ax me later," Nat replied evasively. "I'se gwine dance now." He didn't wait for a reaction but headed toward the circle of dancers and Delia.

His heart sped up. He wasn't sure if it was from seeing her smile warmly at him or knowing that Harry would guess the truth about his decision. When Harry did, Nat knew he was living on borrowed time.

★ ★ ★ ★ ★

Gideon sat silently with his mother and Fletcher, too anxious to sleep because in a few hours there might be a slave uprising. The weapons loaned by the sheriff were close at hand as Gideon watched the hour hand slowly creep around the face of the banjo-shaped clock. It had been his late father's wedding gift to his first wife, Isham's mother.

It wasn't just the excitement of knowing what could happen at dawn that occupied Gideon's thoughts. Tomorrow was the last possible day he could leave for Richmond in time to be at the job interview on Wednesday. He had failed to obtain transportation or the spending money needed for the trip. Even if the revolt was stopped, he couldn't leave. He groaned in silent anguish, still unable to believe his dream was about to die.

★ ★ ★ ★ ★

The evening slipped away, but Nat was reluctant to leave Delia and begin his escape try. He again leaned against the wall closest to the barn door and admired Delia, who made the other slaves whoop in approval.

Nat scowled at the young unmarried men striving to be near her. He was tempted to join them, yet he was aware that although both Harry and Tolliver were now dancing, they were also watching him. He dared not let them catch him alone.

Nat felt a tug at his sleeve and looked down. He recognized the little girl who often carried a heavy bucket of water to the field workers. She didn't speak but slipped a piece of paper into his hand, then ran out the door.

Puzzled, Nat looked around to make sure nobody was watching. Then he nonchalantly turned his back to the dancers and opened his hand. In small, neat script he read, *You will be chained tonight. You are released from your promise. Do what you must to protect yourself.*

There was no signature, but Nat knew Emily had written the note. He stood there, tore the paper into tiny bits, then thrust them deep into his pocket and turned around. Both Harry and Tolliver were gone.

After waiting half an hour in case the men returned, and while Delia was dancing with her back to him, Nat cupped his hand over the bell and slipped outside. He crouched low and scooted along the barn to control his shadow cast by the full moon. Still keeping the bell silent, he removed the collar. Sliding it under an upturned barrel, he silently headed for the river. His heart thudded rapidly as the sound of dancers and music faded behind him. His shadow vanished when he passed under the first trees in the river bottom leading to the swamp. That's when he heard the voices.

★ ★ ★ ★ ★

The tall case clock in the hallway chimed the half hour. "Eleven-thirty," Emily said quietly to Julie. It was long after their usual bedtime, but neither she nor Julie could sleep, knowing what possible horror awaited at dawn. They knew William was also awake in the library when his body servant hurried outside. It was easy for Emily to guess that Levi had been sent to the white overseer, Lewis Toombs, with orders to chain Nat until Travis and Clement would take him away the next day.

That guess was confirmed fifteen minutes later when Levi

rushed back, his eyes wide with excitement. He ran down the hallway toward the library. Seconds later, she heard William's voice explode in anger.

He raced down the hallway, pulling on his jacket and yelling to Levi, "Have my horse saddled and brought around, and light a lantern for me!"

Julie jumped up. "What's the matter?"

"Levi couldn't find Nat, and I know why! He's gone to meet his followers so they can attack us. He won't go far. I'll have Toombs question the dancers while Levi gets Barley Cobb and his hounds. You girls stay inside with the doors locked! I'm going to find Nat and end his troublemaking days forever!"

★ ★ ★ ★ ★

Hearing the voices made Nat quietly drop facedown on the cold, damp ground so they couldn't see him. He peered through some brush to watch three men crouched under a tree out of the moonlight. They blended as one dark, indistinct shadow, but Nat recognized their voices. Julius was instructing Tolliver and Harry. Nat couldn't catch every word, but he heard enough.

When they picked up their hidden weapons, they would first sneak up on Nat in the quarters to make sure he didn't betray them later. Going on to the big house, they would find that Massie, Julie's new maid, had left three downstairs doors unlocked. Inside, Julius, Harry, and Tolliver each had specific assignments.

As Julius began reviewing what each man was to do, Nat slithered away silently. His mind and heart were in turmoil at the two choices suddenly thrust upon him. If he kept running, he might save his own life by escaping to the Underground Railroad.

But if I do that, he reminded himself with a silent groan, *Miss Emily, Gideon, and all of the others will be massacred. That includes my own father and half brother. Can I let them be murdered?*

When Nat was confident that he was far enough away so that the plotters would not hear him, he slowly got to his feet. He stood uncertainly, looking first toward the swamp, then back toward Briarstone. If he kept running, he might escape to freedom. But if he turned back to warn Emily, tomorrow he could be headed for terrible bondage in the South. He had never faced a harder decision.

With a heavy sigh, he made his choice.

The dancers had retired for the night when Nat reached the barn again. He stood in the silent shadows, deeply engrossed in thinking how to warn Emily, when someone stepped out of the shadows into the moonlight.

"There you are!" Delia exclaimed. "Everyone's been looking for you. They've sent for the dogs."

"Oh no!" The words came out as an anguished groan at the sudden twist of fate. Nat grabbed Delia's hand and pulled her back into the barn's shadow. He whispered, "I just overheard Julius, Harry, and Tolliver! They're going to attack the big house at dawn. I've got to warn Miss Emily and the others."

Delia's eyes opened wide in fear. "This dawn?"

"Yes! I need your help!"

Nat's hurried plan was modified by Delia. "No," she whispered when he finished telling her what he planned to do. "You'd take too much risk in entering the big house. I'll do that while you get a horse ready to ride over to her friend's place for help."

"Thanks," Nat replied, "but this is not your problem. I shouldn't have even told you—"

"This is no time to argue!" Delia interrupted, stepping out of the barn's shadows. "I'll get Miss Emily and tell her what you told me about their plans. At least she and the others will be warned and ready."

"Wait!" Nat called in a low, hoarse whisper, but Delia was already running toward the big house. Reluctantly, he headed toward the stables.

★ ★ ★ ★ ★

It was just after midnight when the Tugwell hounds suddenly bawled an alarm.

"Someone's coming!" Gideon yelled, leaping up and seizing one of the borrowed pistols.

Hoofbeats sounded outside as Fletcher snatched up the short

cavalry shotgun and started to blow out the lamp. He stopped when a voice called from outside.

"Gideon! It's Emily!"

"Emily!" Gideon jerked the door open as she halted the horse in the moonlight. Gideon yelled, "Rock! Red! Quiet! Quiet, I say!"

Even before they fully obeyed, Emily's words tumbled out: "Nat just sent word that the attack is at dawn!"

★ ★ ★ ★ ★

The cold night air seeped into Nat's bones as he crouched by the side of the public road a few feet away from the long lane leading to Briarstone's big house. He stared hopefully toward the Tugwell home.

What's taking them so long? he fretted while images of his tense meeting with Emily flickered in his mind.

Delia had seen her standing at the parlor window, gazing anxiously into the moonlight. Emily had responded to Delia's motions and stepped outside. There Emily heard Delia's report from Nat before ducking back inside the house to grab a cloak. Emily insisted Julie stay inside while Emily met with Nat as he led a horse to the door. After a hurried summary of what he had overheard from the plotters, he told her, "You protect yourselves as best you can while I ride to tell Gideon."

"You can't risk it!" Emily had protested. "If the patrollers catch you, they won't believe you. But they won't bother me, and I can bring them to help stop this!"

Nat asked, "Can you ride bareback?"

"I must," she replied. She took the reins from Nat, grabbed a handful of mane, and pulled herself onto the horse's broad back. She turned to Delia, "Thank you for your help, but you'd better get back to your quarters until this is over. Nat, would you please wait at the end of the lane out of sight? I'll be back with Gideon and Mr. Fletcher as soon as possible."

Before Nat could protest, she had ridden off. It seemed like it had been at least half an hour ago, Nat thought as he lay shivering with cold and excitement.

Then he heard hoofbeats and stiffened, his pulse speeding up. *Is it Gideon and Emily—or patrollers?*

HIGH SUSPENSE AT DAWN

Holding his breath, Nat lay motionless on the cold ground until the moonlight revealed a horse with one rider and a mule carrying double coming toward his hiding place. *It must be Emily, Gideon, and the Tugwells' friend,* Nat told himself, releasing his breath.

He stood up as moonlight reflected off of the short-barrelled cavalry shotgun cradled in the crook of John Fletcher's left arm. Emily reined in the horse beside the mule where Nat hurriedly whispered his report.

"There are only three of them. Julius is the leader. He's to enter the front door and climb the main stairs to attack William and his mother in their beds."

"William's not here!" Emily whispered. "He rode off when he heard you'd run away."

"Julius doesn't know that," Nat replied.

"Doesn't matter," Fletcher said softly. "I'll stop him at the front door. What about the other two men?"

Nat explained, "Harry was assigned to the side door, where he is supposed to attack Miss Emily and Miss Julie in the center part of the upstairs. Tolliver has the outside back stairs leading to the third floor."

"That's where Mr. Travis and Clement sleep!" Emily said.

Nat nodded. "I'll take that back door."

Emily, knowing about their blood relationship, looked sharply at him.

He noticed, adding grimly, "I'll protect them."

Emily smiled in the moonlight.

Gideon asked Fletcher, "You want me to take the side door?"

"That would sure help," he replied.

"I'll go with him," Emily volunteered.

"I think you should stay with me," Fletcher suggested.

She answered, "Thanks, but I'd like to help Gideon."

Gideon looked at Fletcher, who hesitated. He was fearful for Emily's safety, but this was no time to express anxiety. "Fine with me. I brought two pistols the sheriff loaned me." He opened his coat to show the weapons in his belt. "You want one, Emily?"

"No, thanks. Give the other to Nat."

Nat shook his head. "You know slaves are never allowed to touch a weapon. I brought a piece of pipe." He produced a two-foot length of pipe from under his coat.

Fletcher cautioned, "That's not much to protect yourself with, Nat. I hope you're good at bluffing."

"I'll have to be."

"All right, then," Fletcher said. "Let's get in position so we'll be ready when the plotters show up."

They left the horse and mule tied at the corner and silently approached the big house on foot, knowing that if they failed in their mission, they could all be dead.

★ ★ ★ ★ ★

The moon had passed its zenith and started dipping low in the west after Gideon and Emily took their posts against the outside brick wall a few feet from the side door. A large evergreen bush grew next to it. Gideon didn't know how long they had remained there, silent as posts, trying to keep from moving so their shadows would not betray their presence.

Emily whispered, "It must be getting close to dawn. Do you think he'll come soon?"

"I think so," Gideon whispered back. His eyes probed the shadows cast by the moon. The crisp autumn air had drained the warmth from his legs until he felt they were turning into wooden stumps. They ached from inactivity, but he couldn't risk unnecessary movement.

Yet that ache was nothing compared to what he felt inside. Even if the Rebellion was stopped, it would be too late for him to get to Richmond. Of course, if he left today, he would make it, but he still had no money and no transportation. It wasn't wise to speak more than necessary, so Gideon agonized in silence while waiting for Harry.

An owl drifting by on silent wings screeched, making Emily jump.

Gideon whispered, "Are you scared?"

"A little." She looked up at him, the moon lighting her golden hair where it showed under her nightcap. "You?"

He was, but didn't want to alarm her. "Naw."

They again fell silent for several minutes. Then, out of the corner of his eye, Gideon glimpsed something flash by overhead and land with a soft thud beyond them.

He gripped Emily's hand. "What was that?"

She joined him in looking toward the front of the house. "Sounded like something fell," she whispered.

Gideon and Emily stood tensely silent, straining to locate the cause of the sound. They didn't hear Harry, who stepped out from behind a tree where he had thrown a stick to distract Gideon and Emily. He had obviously caught sight of them as he stealthily approached the house on his deadly mission. Harry ran silently across the grass and dropped out of sight behind the bush by the door.

★ ★ ★ ★ ★

The moon shining at the back of Briarstone cast shadows on the outside stairs, where they ascended to the third floor. There had been no place close to hide while Nat waited, so he had slipped under the bottom steps to wait for Tolliver. Nat was not concerned about how long he lay in that stiff, cramped position because his troubled thoughts made the time race by.

After what my father and half brother plan to do to me, I don't know why I'm doing this! he told himself. *As for Tolliver, he's coming to kill and burn, so he'll be better armed than I am with this little piece of pipe. Well, if he gets me, at least my own relatives can't sell me into the Deep South!*

A shadow moved off toward the barn, instantly drawing Nat's watchful eyes toward it. A man, crouched low, darted from the barn's shelter toward the carriage house. Nat recognized Tolliver. He carried a hatchet in one hand and a can with a handle in the other.

Probably coal oil to start the fire, Nat told himself, slowly bringing cold-stiffened legs under him so he could jump up when necessary.

He had mixed feelings as Tolliver sprinted from one building to another, nearing the house. Nat thought of how Tolliver must have felt when his two little boys were sold away in spite of Tolliver's tearful pleading to William's father. Nat tried to think how the little boys' mother suffered to die of a broken heart.

But that's no reason to kill people! Nat silently rebuked himself. *My own father and half brother are going to sell me tomorrow, but I can't let Tolliver kill them any more than I could Miss Emily and Gideon!*

Delia's image briefly flitted into Nat's mind, when they had sat side by side in the secret church services. Brother Tynes' words silently echoed in Nat's mind. *"Do good to dem dat . . ."*

Sighing gently, Nat realized that in spite of his outrage over the unfairness of his life, he had a new thought. *No matter how they treat me, I'm not like that.*

His father and half brother had done him a terrible wrong, but that didn't mean he had to repay them evil for evil. His mother had been right about winning being in the mind, but it had been Tynes' message of toleration that had convinced Nat that he was different. He didn't have Uncle George's "glory"—not yet, anyway—but Nat felt as if he had somehow been reborn of a different Father. In spite of the danger approaching him, Nat felt really good.

As Tolliver neared the stairs, Nat gripped his piece of pipe and prepared to act.

★ ★ ★ ★ ★

Emily was tense after vainly waiting to hear or see something toward the front of the house. She leaned close to Gideon to whisper, "What do you think?"

"I guess it was my imagination." He turned around and looked toward the side door just beyond the large bush. The lower part moved slightly. Gideon commented, "The wind's coming up."

Emily drew her cloak tighter around her shoulders. "Oh, I wish this were over!"

"So do I."

They both glanced around, their eyes and ears alert for any sound. Each was shivering slightly, but it was hard to tell whether it was from the cold or excitement. Suddenly a voice was heard from toward the front of the house. Gideon and Emily spun to face that direction.

"That's Mr. Fletcher's voice!" Gideon exclaimed in a hoarse whisper. "But I can't make out his words."

"Neither can I," Emily replied, then whirled around and sucked in her breath. "Gideon, look out!"

He pivoted around just as Harry leaped up from behind the bush and rushed at them with a long club.

★ ★ ★ ★ ★

In back of the house, Tolliver had carefully and quietly mounted the first three steps on the outside stairway. Nat slipped up behind him and pressed a section of pipe against his spine.

Deliberately using proper English to bluff Tolliver into at least momentarily thinking he was a white man, Nat commanded in a low, harsh whisper, "Don't move! I'll take the can! Drop the hatchet and don't turn around!" Nat reached out with his free hand and retrieved the coal oil as Tolliver dropped the hatchet. Nat gulped in relief but kept the pipe pressed against his prisoner. "Don't look back, but step backward down the stairs, very slowly."

When that had been done, Nat gave a push with the pipe. "Good! Now walk around the left side of the house toward the front door. Quietly! Now move!"

★ ★ ★ ★ ★

With his left hand, Gideon shoved Emily aside as Harry rushed forward with his three-foot-long club raised over his head. Gideon yanked a pistol from his belt and yelled, "Stop! Stop right there!"

Harry halted in midstride, still about six feet away from Gideon. For a moment, he glared at them.

"Y'all gwine shoot me if'n I don'?"

Gideon doubted that he could, but he spoke firmly even though goose bumps of fear rippled down his arms. "I'm not going to let you hurt anybody, so drop the club!"

Harry still hesitated, the moonlight striking his face, showing where the branding scar had pulled back his upper lip. He glanced beyond Gideon to Emily.

She said firmly, "You heard him! There are several of us, so drop it!"

Slowly, Harry obeyed.

As the club hit the ground, Gideon darted around in back of his prisoner and ordered, "Now march straight ahead to the front of the house!"

Gideon and Emily walked behind their prisoner toward the sounds of angry voices. Both knew it wasn't over yet.

★ ★ ★ ★ ★

Nat and his prisoner rounded the front of the house from the right just as Gideon and Emily came around from the left with Harry.

Fletcher had his back against the large, ornate front door, facing Julius, who stood between the two Corinthian pillars, holding a broad ax. Fletcher held the cavalry shotgun in his right hand and supported the short barrel with his left forearm, which had no hand. He said sternly, "I'm not going to tell you again! Put it down now!"

Julius obviously was less fearful than his two followers. His broad ax was no match for the shotgun, but he still resisted Fletcher's order.

Emily saw lamps being lit inside the house as other slaves were aroused by the commotion. The door slowly opened a crack. Dark faces peered out as Fletcher stepped aside, keeping his back to the wall.

Julius called out to the house slaves, "Come he'p me! Now's de time to be free!"

Julie's new maid, Massie, stepped out, leaving the door open. "I'se wid y'all," she told Julius.

He yelled triumphantly to other slaves standing in the door. "Dat's de way! Come on, j'ine up wid us."

"No!" Emily cried, leaving Gideon with Harry, and hurried to stand beside Fletcher. "Remember what William told you when the Union soldiers came! How can you live without land, without mules and equipment?"

She pointed toward Julius. "If you join with this man, you'll have to live in the swamp with the snakes and bugs and disease! What will you eat? Where will you find shelter? Where will you run when the hounds follow you? Stay here! Be patient and don't listen to this man!"

Gideon added, "She's right! You want to be free, but not his kind of freedom!"

The house slaves still stood uncertainly in the doorway, not speaking, not moving.

Nat prodded his prisoner up the steps beside the columns. "You've got a choice," he said, forgetting to use dialect. "Stand with Julius and his Rebellion, or stand with us. All who are with us, come stand with me."

Gideon and Emily promptly flanked him while Fletcher covered the conspirators.

For a long moment, there was silence. Then, one by one, the house servants stepped through the open door and took places behind Nat, Gideon, and Emily.

Julius let out an anguished cry, turned quickly, and started running down the long driveway toward the road.

"Don't let him get away!" Gideon cried.

Fletcher replied, "It's all right!" He said to Harry, Tolliver, and Massie, "Go with him if you want!"

Gideon and Emily exchanged startled glances as the insurrectionists ran after Julius. Gideon protested to Fletcher, "Why did you do that? They'll go to our place! My mother's alone!"

"They won't ever get there," Fletcher assured him. "Listen!"

Gideon cocked his head. "Horses! Several of them coming down the public road!"

"Probably patrollers," Fletcher replied, "or maybe the sheriff. But whoever it is, they won't let those runaways get far."

Gideon turned to see Nat reassuring the house slaves who had stood with them.

Emily sighed. "I guess it's finally over."

"Yes, it is," Fletcher agreed. "I'm grateful to God that we're all safe."

Emily added, "I won my wager, so William not only can't sell Nat but he must restore him to service in this house. On the other hand, Gideon, you've lost your chance for that Richmond job."

He took a deep breath before saying, "I know it sounds foolish, but I keep hoping something will still work out."

"So do I," Emily said fervently. "So do I."

★ ★ ★ ★ ★

Travis and Clement had slept through the uprising, so when several patrollers rode up with the four prisoners, Fletcher accompanied them to the barn, where they would be kept under guard until William returned. Then Fletcher climbed the back stairs to report what had happened.

The sun was just brightening the eastern horizon when William returned. Gideon, Emily, Nat, and Julie were talking in front of the house as William looked down from the saddle.

He exclaimed, "You caught him! It's just as well because Cobb is chasing another runaway with his hounds."

Julie protested, "Nat didn't run away, but he saved our lives and kept this place from being burned! Emily, Gideon, tell him about it."

They took turns explaining the details, including how Nat had found the keys to his bell collar and thrown it away, later returning the keys to where he found them. He had started to again run away when he came upon the plotters. But instead of continuing his escape, Nat had returned to warn Emily with the help of a field slave named Delia. Patrollers were now guarding the plotters in the barn.

Emily was surprised that William had listened without interruption. She sensed that one more point had to be strongly made. "William," she said, looking him squarely in the eyes, "if it weren't for Nat's unselfish acts, all of us except you would surely be dead by now, and Briarstone would be burned to the ground."

She took a quck breath and rushed on before he could reply. "William, I'm sorry I made a wager with you, and I won't do it again, but I'm going to hold you to our deal. Nat can't be sold to the slave trader."

William nodded and spoke rapidly. "We're all alive and safe, so I'll keep my word. Nat, I'll go tell Elmo Travis and his son that you're being restored to the big house. Julie, this Delia who helped will replace Massie as your maid. Gideon, I never thought I'd say this, but the least I can do for what you did is provide a carriage, driver, and some spending money so you can make your trip to Richmond. That is, if you can be ready in a few hours."

A broad grin started to spread across Gideon's face, but immediately a doubt sprang to his mind. *What if this is another one of William's plans to get hold of Mama's property while I'm away?* Gideon shook his head. *Stop being so suspicious! Just be grateful.*

"Thanks, William. I'll be ready."

Still, Gideon lingered after William left, and Julie took Nat a few steps away so Gideon and Emily could say their good-byes. Gideon realized he was going to miss her more than he had ever dreamed. But at last he was one step closer to becoming an author.

Emily urged, "Write me from Richmond, and I'll answer. And someday, send me an autographed copy of your first book."

"I will," he promised. "Now I've got to hurry home and get ready—" He stopped as Travis and Clement stepped from behind the house, followed by two male house servants with baggage. A boy approached them leading a horse with a buggy toward the big house.

Gideon and Emily exchanged glances, then quickly moved to stand with Julie and Nat. They all watched as the bags of the departing guests were placed in the buggy. Without looking around, Clement entered the vehicle and sat down. His father started to follow but stopped and glanced toward the four watchers.

Nat didn't lower his eyes, as a slave was expected to do when a white person looked at him. He locked eyes with his father and didn't blink.

As Travis sat down and picked up the reins, Julie whispered, "They're not even going to say thank you for saving their lives!"

Emily didn't answer but glanced at Nat. There was no expression on his face as the buggy passed with Travis and Clement looking straight ahead.

As the sun rose on a new day, Nat kept his chin high, knowing he had proven that he forgave them.

EPILOGUE

From Gideon Tugwell's journal, October 19, 1933

It's been seventy-one years since I recorded what happened to Emily, Nat, and me when the Confederates invaded Maryland and President Lincoln issued his famous Emancipation Proclamation. But it is those personal events on the last Sunday in September 1862 that live in both my journal and my memory.

That same day, I, the boy Gideon, said farewell to my family, Emily, Nat, and the others. I had learned to never give up hope. That helped when I arrived at the Confederate capital in Richmond, where, just before Christmas, totally unexpected adventures plunged me into the battle for Fredericksburg, Virginia.

Emily had about resigned herself to spending the rest of the war in the South, but as the holiday season approached, she became homesick for her native Illinois. Then she received two surprises. She told me later that these, combined with what had happened in September, helped her learn the importance of faith in God, herself, and purpose in life during times of great testing.

Nat revealed to me that he realized life is not always fair, but that each person always has a choice about how to respond to unfairness and also the opportunity to genuinely forgive those who have deeply hurt that individual.

With the second Christmas of the war coming, and Lincoln's freeing of the slaves a week later, Emily, Nat, and I suddenly faced unexpected challenges. Yet no one would have guessed what was going to happen to us individually in the closing days of 1862.

I'll tell you about that when I next open the pages of my journal to relive what it was like to grow up as the terrible War between the States continued.